"What are you doing here?"

Closing the space between them in one stride, Logan took Charlotte's right hand and turned it over. Her mother's class ring glittered in the harsh hospital lighting.

The casual touch did some funny things to her heart. How long had it been since she'd felt a friendly touch? She couldn't remember. Her marriage hadn't been kind to her friendships.

"There was a video online of them taking you to the ambulance, and I saw your mom's ring. You never wore it unless—"

"Unless I was in trouble." She finished the sentence with a watery smile. "I can't believe you remembered."

"I remembered. Whenever that ring showed up on your finger, I knew something was wrong."

He'd known, and he'd always tried to help her. Nobody messed with Logan Carter, and everybody respected him.

Everything just seemed…better when he was around.

Maybe that was why she'd slipped the ring on the day after Dylan's death. Maybe subconsciously she'd been flashing their old signal.

Come help me.

Of course, she'd never expected him to actually show up.

Laurel Blount lives on a small farm in Middle Georgia with her husband, David, their four children, a milk cow, dairy goats, assorted chickens, an enormous dog, three spoiled cats and one extremely bossy goose with boundary issues. She divides her time between farm chores, homeschooling and writing, and she's happiest with a cup of steaming tea at her elbow and a good book in her hand.

Books by Laurel Blount

Love Inspired

A Family for the Farmer
A Baby for the Minister
Hometown Hope
A Rancher to Trust
Lost and Found Faith
Her Mountain Refuge

Visit the Author Profile page at LoveInspired.com.

Her Mountain Refuge

Laurel Blount

LOVE INSPIRED
INSPIRATIONAL ROMANCE

LOVE INSPIRED®
INSPIRATIONAL ROMANCE

ISBN-13: 978-1-335-75931-3

Her Mountain Refuge

For questions and comments about the quality of this book, please contact us at CustomerService@Harlequin.com.

Love Inspired
22 Adelaide St. West, 41st Floor
Toronto, Ontario M5H 4E3, Canada
www.LoveInspired.com

Printed in U.S.A.

My little children, let us not love in word,
neither in tongue; but in deed and in truth.
—*1 John* 3:18

In loving memory of Captain Jerry Torbert of the Lamar County Sheriff's Office, a dedicated public servant and a true and faithful friend.

And in honor of all the law enforcement officers who serve their communities with distinction. May God bless you and keep you safe.

Chapter One

Uh-oh.

Charlotte Tremaine froze midway through buttoning the forty-two tiny buttons scattered up the back of her client's one-of-a-kind wedding gown. Her heart dropped right past her seven-months-and-counting baby bump and hit the overpriced shoes her mother-in-law had insisted she buy for Dylan's funeral.

She gave the gaping fabric a hopeful tug.

Not a chance.

Charlotte's heart started to pound. This was not good.

High society weddings like this one were her only hope of bringing her business out of the red and getting herself and her baby out from under Elizabeth Tremaine's thumb. She'd never enjoyed them, though—and this one was in a class all by itself. This Charlotte's Original was hands-down the most expensive gown she'd designed, and it had given her endless fits. So had the bride, who was one of the most self-centered creatures Charlotte had ever met.

And that was saying something.

Yes, Pippa Sheridan was a gold-plated pain, but her wedding dress was a triumph, if Charlotte did say so herself. It was a sleek dream of heavy satin and handmade

French lace, vintage in its choice of material and refreshingly trendy in its cut and drape.

It was also way, *way* too small.

Biting the inside of her lip, she stared at the perfectly tanned skin bulging between the sides of the bodice. The room was overheated—the ancient church's air conditioners were no match for a muggy Georgia September—but she shivered.

This wasn't going to go over well.

"Hurry up!" Pippa ordered. "The photographer's waiting." The bride glanced in the floor-length mirror, catching Charlotte's eye. Her perfectly feathered brows drew together. "Is something *wrong*?"

Charlotte fumbled for the best way to break this news. The heavy smell of Pippa's exotic bouquet was making her nauseated, and the room had gone a bit wobbly. She stared at her trembling hands, still clutching the fabric, her eye lighting on her late mother's college ring, sparkling on the first finger of her right hand.

Years ago, that ring had been a comforting reminder that help was never far away. Now it was a reminder that she was completely on her own.

She cleared her throat. "You'll need to step out of the dress for a minute."

"Why?"

"I have to make a quick alteration." Charlotte cast an experienced eye down the gap. She'd need a full inch, right here at waist.

She reached to pull down the sleeve, but Pippa's perfectly manicured hand slapped hers away.

"What," the other woman bit out, "is wrong with my dress?"

"It's a little too snug. I'll whip in an extension, right up the back here, and move the buttons." That would take

some time, she realized with a pang. It would also spoil the
line of the dress, which was a shame, but it was the best
she could do in a pinch. "That'll push it up a full size. I
think that'll be enough." She was talking to herself more
than Pippa, just thinking aloud—a habit that had landed
her in trouble more than once.

It got her in trouble again now.

Pippa's eyes narrowed. "Are you implying I've gained
weight?"

Well, yes.

"It happens all the time." Charlotte hurried to assure
her. "Everybody diets before their first fittings, and brides
want their dresses cut as small as possible. Just before the
wedding, there are so many parties, so much rich food, it's
easy to put back on a few pounds. Don't worry. I keep a
sewing kit in my car, and I've pulled off some tricky saves
in my time." Not as tricky as this one, but she'd keep that
part to herself. "Everything will be fine."

She hoped.

Behind them, one of the twelve bridesmaids snickered.
Pippa's face turned an angry red. "I'm the same size I've
always been."

Oh, boy. "If you'll just step out of the dress…"

"You made a mistake, and you don't want to admit it.
This is your fault!"

Wasn't everything always her fault? Or it had been,
for years now, ever since she'd married into the Tremaine
family. Dylan's drinking, his gambling, the abuse—all of
it had been Charlotte's fault.

Including Dylan's death, at least according to Elizabeth Tremaine.

The room was so hot, and Pippa's perfume fought with
the heavy smell of the flowers. Charlotte swallowed hard,
and her knees began to shake.

Please, Lord, don't let me pass out. That had happened before during this pregnancy, when her blood pressure went too high. Her doctor had warned her repeatedly about reducing her stress, but nobody working society weddings—or living with Elizabeth—could avoid stress. It came with the territory.

The thought of her disapproving mother-in-law sent Charlotte's pounding heartbeat into a new gear. The Sheridans were country club friends of the Tremaines. Elizabeth was already seated out there in one of the festooned pews, impeccably dressed as always, waiting for the wedding of the year to get started.

She'd made it clear to Charlotte that this dress needed to be perfect. *If you can't handle this level of dressmaking, you shouldn't attempt it. The Sheridans hired you because of our connection, and I don't want to be embarrassed.*

Of course, no matter how perfect the dress was, Elizabeth would pick it apart afterward, using that bored, amused voice that sounded so soft but cut hearts like steel.

Charlotte clenched her fingers on the back of a dainty chair. She'd been praying for the strength to stand up for herself. Since her marriage, her heart and her self-confidence had been stomped flat so many times she'd lost count. But that chapter of her life was over, and now she had her baby to consider. She'd promised God—and herself—that she was going to stop cringing in front of these people. This wasn't her fault, and she needed to make that clear.

It might have helped, though, if she could have managed a deep breath.

"The dress fit perfectly when you tried it on for me last." Her ears were buzzing. "I told you," she went on doggedly. "Not a good idea to do the final fitting so far out. Two weeks, I told you, so we could be sure. But you were going to Paris with your bridesmaids, remember, and you didn't want to—"

"Oh, shut up! Madison, go get Mother," Pippa snapped. A bridesmaid scurried out of the room. "She's going to be livid."

No doubt. Charlotte winced. Daphne Sheridan was every bit as difficult to deal with as Elizabeth.

"I can fix it," she murmured desperately.

Pippa leaned in close, her angry face strangely blurry. "You'd better. I don't care if you are some poor, pitiful widow. If you ruin my wedding, Charlotte Tremaine, I will ruin *you*. Do you hear me?"

Charlotte tried to answer, but the buzzing in her ears was too loud, and big black spots danced in front of Pippa's face. The world tilted, and the spots expanded until there was nothing but darkness.

At quarter till five, Sheriff Logan Carter parked his patrol car underneath the fluttering leaves of the pecan tree outside his office and frowned at a familiar blue pickup.

What was Ruby doing here?

It was probably nothing. His elderly foster mom liked to keep a close eye on all her grown-up kids, and she knew she was always welcome in his office.

Still, as he walked up the sidewalk past the flagpole, his instincts prickled.

Things had been too quiet lately, even for Cedar Ridge. For the past week, Logan hadn't had to phone the coroner, the ambulance or the fire department—not once. In fact, the Roane County deputies hadn't issued so much as a speeding ticket. All the citizens of his beloved town were safe, well and—as far as he knew, anyway—behaving themselves.

It had Logan's nerves on edge.

Years of law enforcement and a childhood in and out of the Georgia foster care system had taught him that quiet spells were generally followed by some kind of blowup. He sensed that Ruby's visit was about to send his peaceful week right down the drain.

Trouble—any kind of trouble—was the last thing he needed two months before an election. As things stood now, Logan was expected to win by a comfortable margin, in spite of his refusal to waste his time campaigning.

He didn't have time to go around glad-handing with local politicians at pancake breakfasts. He'd served as sheriff for four years. The way he saw it, the citizens of Cedar Ridge could vote based on his record.

But public opinion could turn on a dime, and his oily opponent Barton Myers would be quick to grab any advantage he could. The idea made Logan's gut clench, but he took a breath and sent up his standard prayer.

You're in charge, Lord. Just give me my orders and the strength to carry them out. Then he pushed through the glass door into the office.

Ruby sat behind the counter in the intake area. Her glasses were perched on the end of her nose, and she was peering at the computer. Marla Shaunessy, the middle-aged dispatcher he'd inherited from the previous sheriff, hovered nearby.

"Finally." His foster mom spoke without glancing up. "I was about to make Marla here call you on the radio."

Logan grinned. She'd have done it, too. "Good to see you, too, Ruby. What brings you to town?"

"A haircut appointment, but that ain't what you want to know. You want to know why I'm here pestering you. Everybody at the beauty parlor was yammering about this video on the *Georgia Talks* page so I came over to take a look at it."

"Sorry, Sheriff," Marla interjected. "I told her the computers aren't for personal use, but—"

"But I didn't pay one jot of attention." Ruby tapped a key, frowned and leaned closer to the screen.

"It's okay, Marla." Very few people were allowed to bend Sheriff Carter's rules, but Ruby Sawyer was one of them. "I'll keep an ear out for the radio for a few minutes. Why don't you have a cup of coffee in the break room?"

"Yes, sir." Throwing one last worried look at the woman occupying her chair, Marla disappeared down the hallway.

"What's got the ladies at Cindy's Cuts stirred up today?" Logan riffled through a stack of mail while his foster mom made tsking noises at the computer. "Whatever's on that screen, I'd take it with a grain of salt. *Georgia Talks* is the online version of those magazines at the supermarket checkout. It's mostly nonsense."

"Mostly nonsense ain't *all* nonsense." His mom shook her head. "It's not *what's* on here that's bothering me. It's *who*."

Logan frowned. "One of us?" Ruby's family of six former foster kids were a tight-knit group. Surely he'd have heard if someone was in trouble.

"Not this time. It's that sweet high school friend of yours, Charlotte Moore." Ruby sighed. "Charlotte Tremaine's her married name. Bless her heart, she's in a real mess."

"Charlotte?" His normally steady heart did a series of quick, hard beats. He hadn't seen Charlotte for…what had it been, now? Two-three years? Not since she'd married that snotty Savannah rich boy Dylan Tremaine. "What's happened?"

"That husband of hers is dead, for starters. Crashed his car into some store building, running from the police, driving drunk." She made a disgusted noise. "I know it's not right to speak ill of the dead, but I can't say I'm surprised. That boy had a shifty-eyed look. I always wondered why Charlotte took up with him."

Because Charlotte never could resist somebody who needed her help. Logan didn't speak his thought aloud. Instead, he said, "When?"

"Five months ago or better. Left that poor girl expecting their first baby." Ruby clucked her tongue. "She must be six, seven months along, I'm guessing, going by this video."

Charlotte was pregnant? Logan's heart jolted again. "What video?"

"See for yourself."

Logan dropped the mail and rounded the reception counter. He leaned over Ruby's shoulder to look at the computer screen—and felt as if somebody had kicked him squarely in the gut.

The video was frozen on a candid photo taken at some society event. Was that really Charlotte? The pale woman on Marla's computer screen didn't look much like the free-spirited girl who'd been his first friend in Cedar Ridge—and his best friend for years after that.

They'd met on his first day at the high school, when she'd plopped herself down at his lonely lunch table. He'd just been shifted to a new foster home, which had meant a different school and the loss of his hard-won spot on his previous school's baseball team. He'd been feeling miserable and sullen, and he hadn't wanted to talk to anybody, much less this too-pretty girl in a weird, eye-popping outfit.

But the pretty girl couldn't take a hint, so finally he'd said rudely, *Are you always this annoying?*

And instead of getting mad, she'd laughed. *Always,* she'd assured him. Her honesty had appealed to him as much as her sassy smile. Then she'd stolen the cookie off his lunch tray and taken a big bite.

They'd been friends from that moment on. And *always* had become their inside joke—a kind of shorthand for their friendship.

Back then Charlotte had worn her blond hair in a messy ponytail, and when she got bored, she'd stain the tips with magic marker. Pink, purple, green, blue. She'd gone through the whole rainbow one summer, a shade at a time. She'd worn colorful outfits she designed herself, often repurposing items she picked up at the local thrift shop. Because she was Charlotte Moore, the granddaughter of local textile mill magnate Ronald Moore, she'd gotten away with it.

This woman's hair was sleeked up into a fancy-looking twist, and she wore an elegant dress and a circlet of pearls.

Pearls.

"Are you sure this is Charlotte?" He leaned in, looking hard. Yeah, that was Charlotte, all right. He recognized that cute little tip-up at the end of her nose, and her eyes were the same blue-green, although now there were worry wrinkles in their corners.

"Says so, later in the video. You going to watch it or not?" Ruby prompted impatiently.

"Hold your horses." He tapped the triangle to make the video play.

Charlotte's picture was replaced by wobbly footage of an ambulance parked outside a church festooned with white ribbons. Lights strobed as paramedics bumped a stretcher down the wide steps, and Logan caught a glimpse of a round, pregnant stomach shrouded by the sheet.

An invisible narrator spoke breathlessly. "Crispy Cracker heiress Pippa Sheridan's Savannah wedding took an unexpected turn when bridal gown designer Charlotte

Tremaine collapsed during an altercation with the bride. According to witnesses, Ms. Sheridan's eight-thousand-dollar dress was not properly fitted, causing a last-minute emergency." The stretcher rolled closer on its way to the ambulance, but the paramedics blocked the cameras.

"Mrs. Tremaine, who is over seven months pregnant, was taken to Memorial Hospital as a precautionary measure. Although her doctor has declined to comment, sources say the mother-to-be is under a great deal of stress since her husband's death."

The paramedics shifted to lift the gurney into the ambulance. Charlotte's face still wasn't visible, but Logan tapped the Pause button.

"What?" Ruby demanded.

He didn't answer. He zoomed in on Charlotte's right hand, trailing off the stretcher. The enlarged picture was blurry, but it was clear enough for him to recognize the ring on her finger.

She was wearing her mother's ring.

He straightened, unable to take his eyes off the screen. "I have to go to Savannah."

Ruby studied him. "You planning to tell me what's going on?"

"As soon as I know myself."

"I guess that'll have to do." The elderly woman rose to her feet with a soft grunt. "Call and let me know you got there safe, you hear? And give Charlotte my best."

"I will." As Ruby made her way to the door, Logan raised his voice. "Marla, radio Benji and tell him I'll be 10-6 until further notice. Probably at least a day. Maybe two."

"You're going off duty for two days?" Marla poked her head through the doorway. "You never do that."

"I'll have my cell, so he can call if he gets into anything sticky. He should be fine, but notify Sheriff Tanner in Sussex County that I'm out of town, just in case." When Marla didn't respond, he lifted an eyebrow. "All right?"

Her eyes were wide. "Sheriff, this isn't like you. What's wrong?"

"No idea." His eyes strayed back to the frozen computer screen. "But I intend to find out."

Savannah was a six-hour drive from Cedar Ridge, so Logan went home and swapped his patrol car for his truck. He considered changing out of his uniform, too, but in the end, he decided against it. He wasn't sure what he'd face in Savannah, and a sheriff had statewide jurisdiction. If his uniform would afford him any professional courtesies, he wouldn't turn them down.

He merged smoothly onto the interstate, settling in for the duration. Traffic wasn't heavy, and his mind drifted to the last time he'd seen Charlotte.

She'd come home from the Savannah College of Art and Design with Dylan in tow for her grandmother's eightieth birthday. Logan had taken a dislike to the arrogant guy on sight, and as soon as he'd been able to get Charlotte off to herself, he'd peppered her with worried questions.

He loved the girl to death—he always had. But her soft heart tended to overrule her good judgment, and when that happened, he made it his business to step in. Logan's tough childhood had given him two gifts, an unflinching devotion to honesty and the ability to sniff out a liar at fifty paces.

This Dylan Tremaine was definitely a liar and unless Logan missed his guess, a bully, too. When he'd hinted as much, Charlotte had grown defensive. She'd told him Dylan's sob story—domineering mother, dead father, lonely, misunderstood rich kid with a passion for art.

Logan had rolled his eyes. He didn't believe a word of

that, and for some reason, Charlotte's unquestioning devotion to this college boy had annoyed him. So he'd been a little too blunt, and for the first time in their long friendship, they'd argued.

Fine, he'd told her, frustrated. *But when you get your heart broken—and I guarantee you, you will—don't come crying to me.*

She must have taken him at his word. He hadn't heard from her for months, not until she'd sent him an invitation to her wedding. It was all fancy, printed with some sort of raised ink, but with one word handwritten on it.

Always.

He'd stared at it for a solid hour. Then he'd politely declined.

Since then, he'd heard nothing. Her grandparents had died not long after the wedding, one right after the other. The services had been held out of town. The house was sold off by an agent, and Charlotte had never come back to Cedar Ridge.

Which meant what he was doing right now didn't make a whole lot of sense.

But he was doing it anyway.

He pulled into the hospital parking lot just after eleven. Visiting hours were long over, but his uniform—and a little charm—got him past the nurses' desk. A few minutes later he was standing in the doorway of Charlotte's room.

She was asleep, hooked up to some sort of blinking monitor, her hair tousled over the pillow. She looked fragile, vulnerable—and even more pregnant in person, which jolted him. She also seemed awfully alone. There were no flowers in the room, no silly stuffed bears, no cards.

No evidence that anybody cared about her at all.

He stepped closer. Even in sleep, Charlotte's forehead was creased, and the hand wearing her mother's ring cupped protectively over her rounded tummy. In the corners of her eyes, he saw those new, worried grooves—and streaks of dried tears.

The last words he'd ever spoken to her echoed in his mind.

Don't come crying to me.

Well, she hadn't. But here he was.

He stood silently, watching her sleep. He'd only intended to lay eyes on her—to scope out the situation as best he could. Then he'd planned on finding a cheap hotel someplace and coming back to the hospital first thing in the morning.

But now, looking at Charlotte lying alone in this sterile room, he tossed that plan out the window. Moving soundlessly, he picked up a metal chair, set it just inside the door and settled down to wait out the night.

Chapter Two

Charlotte Tremaine drifted up from a heavy sleep, slowly becoming aware of the noises and smells around her. She stayed very still as she tried to figure out where she was.

Hospital.

In her experience hospitals had been unhappy places, full of death and grief. Her heartbeat sped up as fear kicked in. Had something happened to the baby? She kept her eyes closed, forcing herself to take the deep, calming breaths her doctor had been recommending. Her unborn son shifted position under her hand, and she relaxed at the familiar sensation. As far as she could tell, he was fine.

That was good.

Everything else, not so much.

Memories filtered in, each one worse than the last. That awful gap between the pretty, sparkling buttons. Pippa's perfectly made up, furious face.

She must have fainted, and worst of all, she'd passed out before she'd fixed the dress. She knew Pippa's threat hadn't been an idle one. The minute she got back from her honeymoon, she'd make it her mission to destroy Charlotte's business—if she hadn't done that already.

As sick as Charlotte was of dealing with society brides,

her pulse stuttered at the thought. Charlotte's Originals had to succeed. Dylan's gambling had left her mired in financial quicksand. Without a reliable income, she wouldn't be able to move out of Elizabeth's home, wouldn't be able to raise her own son as she saw fit.

That couldn't happen. She had to figure out how to fix this. As Charlotte started brainstorming damage control, she heard a noise.

Somebody was in the room.

Please, Lord, don't let it be Elizabeth.

She lifted an eyelid, scanning the room through a fringe of lashes. A broad-shouldered man in a rumpled khaki uniform was asleep in a chair by the door. His legs were stretched out in front of him, his arms crossed over his chest.

She opened her eyes fully, zeroing in on the man's profile, the straight blade of a nose, the strong jaw, the dark hair, cropped short. Her heart lifted as recognition dawned.

"Logan?" Charlotte pushed herself upright in the bed, causing a monitor to beep loudly.

He opened his eyes, his tired face easing into a smile. "Look who's finally awake."

"What are you—" she started. Before she could finish, her ob-gyn, Dr. Alice Edwards, poked her head in the door.

"Good morning, Charlotte." The doctor raised an eyebrow and gave Logan a thorough once-over. "And you are?"

"A very old friend," Charlotte supplied before he could answer. "Logan Carter. He's from my hometown in North Georgia."

"I see. Welcome to Savannah, Sheriff." The gray-haired physician came in and tapped a button to shut off the alarm. "Do you want him to step outside while we talk or is he okay to stay?"

"He can stay." She still couldn't believe Logan was really here, and she didn't want to let him out of her sight.

"All right." Dr. Edwards looked down at Charlotte, her face serious. "You gave us quite a scare yesterday, young lady. I hate to say I told you so, but you know I did."

Only the somber look on her doctor's face could have distracted her from Logan. "Is my baby all right?"

"Right as rain, no thanks to you. You were having contractions when you came in, but they stopped before I had to step in. Plenty of rest and no stress. That's what I said after that last incident." Dr. Edwards tsked her tongue. "But what did you do? You worked that circus of a Sheridan wedding. Not a good call, Charlotte. You should be thankful you're no worse off than you are."

"If the baby's okay, why does she need an IV?"

Startled, Charlotte glanced at Logan. He'd asked the question as if he had a perfect right to, as if this weren't the first time she'd seen him in years. She should probably have felt annoyed, but instead, grateful tears welled up in her eyes.

At least somebody cared enough to ask.

"The IV's nothing to worry about. Just some fluids." Dr. Edwards turned back to Charlotte. "You were dehydrated. That's partly why you collapsed. The other part is your blood pressure, which you need to take more seriously." The physician put her hands on her hips. "I can get the discharge paperwork ready, but only if you give me your word you're actually going to rest, monitor your blood pressure daily and stay hydrated. Let other people pamper you for a while. Absolutely no more weddings and as little stress as possible. Am I making myself clear?"

"Yes," Charlotte murmured. "I'll try to take it easy." She'd do her best, but she wasn't sure how she'd manage it. She'd been praying for some kind of relief, but God was taking His own sweet time answering.

"You'd better do more than try. We don't want this baby coming early, and this was a near miss. If you're a real friend, you'll make sure she behaves herself," she told Logan as she walked past him. "Has she always been this stubborn?"

Logan looked at Charlotte while politely pushing open the door for the doctor. Their eyes met, and the corner of his mouth tilted up. "Always."

At the word, a tidal wave of bittersweet memories crashed over her. As hard as it was to believe, Logan had come. He was really here.

She drank in the sight of him, noting the changes. He was broader across the chest than he'd been as a teenager. There was a nonnegotiable set to his shoulders and a new, self-assured tilt to his chin. He'd come a long way from the lanky loner she'd befriended in the high school cafeteria.

"How did you…?" she whispered once Dr. Edwards was gone. "What are you doing here?"

Closing the space between them in one stride, he took her right hand and turned it over. Her mother's class ring glittered in the harsh hospital lighting.

The casual touch, like his take-charge question earlier, did some funny things to her heart. How long had it been since she'd felt a friendly touch? She couldn't remember. Her marriage hadn't been kind to her friendships.

She swallowed and tried to focus on what he was saying.

"There was a video online of them taking you to the ambulance, and I saw your mom's ring. You never wore it unless—"

"Unless I was in trouble." She finished the sentence with a watery smile. "I can't believe you remembered."

"I remembered. Whenever that ring showed up on your finger, I knew something was wrong."

He'd known, and he'd always tried to help her, if he could. Mostly, they'd laughed about it, but there'd been once or twice when he'd gotten her out of a truly sticky spot. Nobody messed with Logan Carter, and everybody respected him. He had a way of diffusing situations just by showing up.

Everything just seemed...better when he was around.

Maybe that was why she'd slipped the ring on the day after Dylan's death. Maybe subconsciously, she'd been flashing their old signal.

Come help me.

Of course, she'd never expected him to actually show up.

"So?" Logan released her hand and sat in the chair closest to her bed. "You going to tell me what's going on?" His face shifted. "I mean, apart from the obvious. I'm sorry about Dylan, Charlotte. I didn't even know he'd passed away until yesterday."

"You never liked him." *And you were right.*

Logan didn't deny it. "I'm still sorry. You cared about him, and I care about you."

"You must." She shook her head. "It's a long drive from Cedar Ridge, and you're in your uniform so you came straight from work. Then you sat up in a chair all night. I just...can't believe you did that for me after—" She broke off before finishing, "All these years."

After you warned me about Dylan, and I wouldn't listen. That's what she'd nearly said. Logan had told her she'd be on her own when things got bad, that he wouldn't be running to her rescue anymore.

She'd believed him. Logan always meant what he said.

"You looked like you needed a friend." He lifted one

eyebrow, his dark eyes searching hers. "Look, Charlotte, I don't know what all's going on with you. Well," he nodded toward her baby bump with a smile, "obviously I can figure out some of what's going on. Maybe we didn't end things on the best note, and we haven't kept in touch, but you were my friend back when I needed one. You tell me what the trouble is, and I'll help you any way I can."

He spoke matter-of-factly. In Logan's straight-and-narrow mind, she realized, his offer made perfect sense.

She'd forgotten men like this existed.

"Your assistance won't be necessary, Officer." Elizabeth Tremaine advanced into the room, shooting Charlotte an icy glare.

What an embarrassment.

She didn't say the words aloud, but she didn't have to. Charlotte knew that look all too well. "I'm sorry you've wasted your trip, but I've already made myself very clear with your superiors. Any questions about my late son should be addressed to our attorney, and his widow certainly doesn't require any help from law enforcement."

This must be Charlotte's mother-in-law. Logan watched Charlotte's expression change as the older woman approached her.

Charlotte didn't like this woman. That was all he needed to know—for now.

"I'm not here in an official capacity, Mrs. Tremaine. Charlotte and I are old friends. I saw her collapse on the news, so I came to check on her."

"I see." The older woman turned toward him, her eyes narrowed. "Well, that was thoughtful of you, but as you can see, Charlotte's not up to entertaining visitors."

Logan met the frosty blue gaze with a calm stare of his own, one he'd found particularly effective at getting people to think twice about testing him. Mrs. Tremaine, however, didn't blink, and she didn't break eye contact either. This, he realized, was a woman very much used to getting her own way.

"Excuse me for a minute, Charlotte," he said easily. Then he nodded at Dylan's mother. "Ma'am."

Ten minutes later he was back, Dr. Edwards in tow. He opened the hospital door without knocking, interrupting Elizabeth in midtirade.

"The dress was an absolute disaster, Charlotte, and calling Pippa fat on her wedding day in front of her bridesmaids certainly didn't help. Why are you always so tactless?"

Charlotte's face was white, her mouth was trembling and her hands were crossed protectively over her body. Logan frowned.

Victim's stance. He saw it way too often in his line of work—and he hated it when he did. He turned to Dr. Edwards, but apparently he wasn't the only one who knew how to read this situation. She was moving toward the bed, her face set in stern lines.

"Mrs. Tremaine, would you please step outside with me?"

"Dr. Edwards." Charlotte's mother-in-law studied the doctor without budging. "It's about time. How soon can my daughter-in-law be discharged?"

"We need to discuss a few things first. I'm very concerned about Charlotte."

"Why?" Elizabeth's eyes narrowed. "Is something wrong with the baby?"

The baby, Logan noticed. Not Charlotte. Just the baby.

"Not yet, but if Charlotte's blood pressure doesn't stay down, there certainly could be. She needs peace and quiet. And," the doctor added, "absolutely no stress." She shot a loaded look at Mrs. Tremaine, who returned it without flinching.

"Fine. Charlotte can stay in seclusion in my home until the baby's born." She glanced at a thin gold watch on her wrist. "Can we possibly hurry this process up? I have a luncheon."

"Do you want to go home with her, Charlotte?" Logan asked.

Mrs. Tremaine turned, lifting an eyebrow as if she hadn't realized he was still in the room. She didn't look pleased.

Logan ignored her. He saw Charlotte's breathing ramp up as she darted an uneasy look at her mother-in-law. Then she looked back at him, pleading silently.

Don't make me tell the truth.

He was putting her between a rock and a hard place. He knew that, but he didn't see much way around it. He wanted to help her, but she was going to have to do her part.

"Do you want to go home with this woman and stay there until the baby's born?" He repeated his question clearly.

"Oh, for—" Mrs. Tremaine started off, but Logan interrupted.

"Please be quiet, ma'am. Charlotte?"

Charlotte had never lied to him, not once. She knew how it wounded him when people told him anything other than the absolute truth.

She also knew why.

"No," she whispered.

All eyes in the room turned to her. She sat stiffly in the bed, her face pale, her hands still clasped protectively over the mound of her baby bump.

"Excuse me?" Mrs. Tremaine asked icily after a stretched-out silence.

"I'm sorry, Elizabeth, but I'd rather not stay with you."

Logan had spent years picking the truth out of situations where everybody seemed inclined to hide it. He took note of the relevant details, one by one.

Charlotte appeared determined, but she was also terrified. Her breathing was too quick, and her body was tense.

Dr. Edwards looked relieved. She hadn't liked the idea of Charlotte staying at the Tremaine home, either.

Elizabeth Tremaine only looked irritated.

"Of course you're staying with me, Charlotte. Where else could you possibly go?"

"With me." Logan spoke up. "Charlotte can come back to Cedar Ridge with me and stay on my mother's farm for a nice, long visit. It's a quiet place, way up in the mountains. Peaceful. No stress. It'll be perfect."

He used a tone he'd found useful in law enforcement. Absolutely certain and completely calm. Act like you know what you're doing—and that you have the authority to do it—and nine people out of ten will go along.

He wasn't surprised to discover that Elizabeth Tremaine was the tenth person.

"That," she said, "is out of the question."

"I think it's a great idea," Dr. Edwards said firmly. "Charlotte needs to rest, and I often advise my patients to go away from home for that. Less temptation to fiddle with work." She turned to Logan. "Is there an obstetrician in this mountain town of yours?"

"Sure is. My younger sister just had her first baby, and she had no complaints about her care."

"I'll need some contact information. Charlotte should be monitored, but if there's a good local doctor, that won't be a problem."

"It's a ridiculous idea." For the first time, Mrs. Tremaine looked alarmed. "Charlotte, you can't seriously be considering such a thing."

"The mountains," Charlotte murmured. "I love the mountains in the fall when the leaves start to turn." She looked up at Logan and smiled. "The colors are always so beautiful, like a big patchwork quilt has been flung over the hills."

He smiled back at her. That sounded like the Charlotte he remembered.

"Sounds like a plan." Dr. Edwards nodded at Logan on her way out the door. "Call your sister and get that doctor's name and number. I'll start the discharge paperwork."

"Wait just a minute," Mrs. Tremaine spluttered. "There's no way I'm allowing—"

Logan cut her off. "Ma'am, with all due respect, your daughter-in-law is a mentally competent adult. There's nothing here for you to allow." He spoke in a tone that brooked no argument. "She's made her decision. She's leaving this hospital with me, and that's the end of it."

Mrs. Tremaine set her jaw and stared him down. "She may leave here with you, but I assure you, Sheriff. That will *not* be the end of it."

Logan didn't doubt that she meant it, but at the moment he didn't care.

Charlotte was smiling. That was all that mattered to him.

Chapter Three

Later that evening, Logan rolled his truck to a stop in front of his foster mom's farmhouse. He glanced at Charlotte, slumped against the passenger window. She'd fallen asleep just north of Atlanta, and even the bumpy drive up Sawyer's mountain hadn't woken her.

That was good because before he invited her in, he had one pesky detail to take care of. Ruby had no idea they were coming. He'd meant to call ahead, but he'd been so caught up in looking after Charlotte that he'd forgotten about it until they were halfway here. He'd decided to wait, figuring it would be easier to explain everything in person. Leaving the truck idling, he cleared the porch steps in two strides.

He followed his nose through the house to the kitchen. Ruby stood at the counter, sprinkling flour onto a piece of cube steak. Oil was heating in her cast-iron skillet, and green beans bubbled on the stove. He smelled biscuits baking and knew without asking that there'd be enough of everything to share.

There always was.

He could tell by the set of Ruby's shoulders that she

knew he was behind her, but she didn't say anything. She waited for him to speak first.

That little trick—and many others—had served her well when she'd been raising her brood. Branded "hard-to-place" by the foster care system, Ruby's six kids were more challenging than most, but they'd met their match in this plain-spoken woman. She'd refused to be put off by their checkered pasts, welcoming them into her home with open arms—and an equally open heart.

Logan had come to Ruby's after his father had been popped for rooking an elderly couple out of their savings. It was a familiar routine. Logan's mother had hit the wind years ago, so whenever affable con man Martin Carter went to jail, his son was chucked into foster care. Over the years, he'd had eight placements and some bad experiences, so he'd arrived at Sweet Springs Farm with a giant-sized chip on his shoulder.

He'd been lied to by pretty much everybody he'd ever met, so he made it a strict policy to trust nobody. He'd held out on Ruby for months, but eventually, he'd discovered that this scrawny old lady actually meant it when she told him he was part of her family for good.

He cleared his throat. "Ruby, I need a favor."

"Mmm?" She glanced over her shoulder. "This favor got something to do with the reason you hightailed it to Savannah yesterday?" She dredged the meat in the flour and picked up the pepper shaker. "Speaking of that, how's Charlotte doing?"

"Not so good." Logan shifted his weight from one shoe to the other. He felt like a teenager asking for the car keys. "She's having trouble with her pregnancy, her doc is worried and her mother-in-law's a real piece of work. So, I brought her home. I'm sorry. I should have called first, but…she's outside in my truck, and she needs a place to stay. A quiet place, where she can rest for a while. Maybe a few weeks. I wondered if—"

"'Course that child can stay here," Ruby interrupted. "For as long as she likes."

Relieved, Logan grabbed Ruby in a firm hug, lifting her right off her orthopedic shoes. She chuckled, batting at him with a floury hand.

"Mind that grease, son. It's hot. Now you go get her while I finish up here. We'll have us some supper and get everything worked out."

When he stepped back onto the porch, Charlotte was standing beside the truck gazing out at the mountains. She glanced at him and smiled wearily.

"I'd forgotten how pretty it is up here."

"Yeah." He looked around with affection. Sweet Springs Farm nestled in a hollow between the mountains, higher than the town, but well sheltered by the surrounding peaks. Old trees stood silent guard around the house—oaks and pines, dogwood and laurel. "It'll get prettier. The leaves haven't started turning yet, but they will before much longer."

"It's beautiful now, too. All those different shades of green. There must be a thousand of them. And just smell that fresh, clean air. It's a wonderful place, Logan, it really is."

Logan agreed with her, but he knew other folks wouldn't have. The scenery might be spectacular, but Ruby's little farm was as plain and homely as she was herself. The white clapboard house was surrounded by a scattering of weathered outbuildings that sheltered her collection of rescue animals. A red clay path wound up the mountain to the original Sawyer log cabin, now kept by Ruby as a rental property. Both the farm and the cabin had been allowed to remain when the forest had been converted into a national park, so Ruby had no near neighbors.

It was remote, and it sure wasn't fancy, but this old farm had been the first safe place Logan had ever known, and it meant a lot to him. Which was why, as an adult, he'd dedicated himself to keeping it, Ruby and the town of Cedar Ridge as safe as he possibly could.

He offered her his arm. "Ruby's got supper cooking. I hope you're hungry."

She should be. She hadn't eaten much breakfast, but Logan hadn't faulted her for that. Hospital food wasn't exactly five-star cuisine. But he hadn't been able to get her to eat lunch, either, although he'd offered to stop wherever she wanted. She'd asked only for a vanilla milkshake, and she'd left most of that melting in the cup holder of his truck.

He was no expert on pregnant women, but even he knew they needed to eat.

To his relief, she said, "I'm starving, but I hope Ruby didn't go to any extra trouble."

"No trouble at all, honey." Ruby appeared, opening her screen door wide. "It's a treat to see you. Come on in, 'cause everything's just about ready. Mind her on those steps there, son. They aren't as even as they could be."

Charlotte sniffed as they walked inside. "Something smells good," she said, and Logan relaxed.

She'd eat now, all right. Nobody could resist Ruby's cooking.

Charlotte insisted on helping set the table, though both he and Ruby urged her to sit and put her feet up. When they were finally seated, the simple food steaming on the table in front of them, Ruby reached out, taking his and Charlotte's hands in hers.

"I'll say grace," she announced. "Go on, children. Grab hands."

After a second's hesitation, he took Charlotte's free hand in his.

"I thank You, Lord, for the food on this table," Ruby said, "and for bringing these good folks to sit with me around it. In Jesus's name, amen."

Logan smothered a smile. Ruby always got straight to the point, even with God.

"So, honey." His foster mother nudged the basket of hot biscuits toward Charlotte. "When are you due?"

"November third."

He did some quick calculations in his head. Not quite two more months. He noticed Charlotte was looking at him funny, and he realized he was still holding her hand.

"Sorry," he muttered, releasing it. Ruby studied him, a forkful of green beans halfway to her mouth. A sharp interest sparked into her eyes.

But all she said was, "Well, a brand-new baby coming at that time of year will be a blessing for you. For Dylan's mama too, I reckon. The first holidays over a grave are the hardest. This little one will be a comfort to both of you, I'm sure."

If he hadn't been watching closely, he'd have missed Charlotte's quick wince. "My mother-in-law's very excited about the baby. These biscuits are amazing, Ruby. You'll have to let me copy your recipe."

"Oh, I don't write nothing down, but I'll show you how to make 'em while you're here," Ruby said. "I don't imagine you've had time to study up on cooking. You've been running a sewing business, haven't you?"

"That's right." As they ate, Charlotte chatted about her experiences designing custom wedding dresses. Ruby seemed fascinated, but Logan wasn't really listening.

His law enforcement brain had been triggered by that quick play of expressions over Charlotte's face at the mention of her husband and his mother. He already knew her mother-in-law wasn't anything to brag about, but he got the feeling that was just the tip of this iceberg.

"What about Dylan? Was he excited about the baby, too?"

He asked the questions without thinking, interrupting a story Charlotte was telling about some dress she'd designed for a wedding involving a hot-air balloon. Both Ruby and Charlotte stared at him.

"Oh!" Charlotte stammered, flushing. "Well—"

"Surely he must have been. A first baby's pretty big news." He watched her carefully while he waited for her response.

"Logan, stop badgering." Ruby shot a warning look over the rim of her iced tea glass. "You ain't on duty, and you don't want to upset her."

"I'm not upset," Charlotte assured her. "Logan's been so kind. I really appreciate his help—and yours. Are you sure you're comfortable with me staying here?"

"Don't be silly," Ruby said. "If you're done eating, why don't you go take a look at your room? Second door on the left. I'd like a private word with my boy here. Won't take a minute."

"Of course." Charlotte rose, placing her napkin neatly on the table. "I can't remember when I've enjoyed a better supper, Ruby. Thank you."

"Oh, honey. You're mighty welcome." Ruby watched her leave the room, then turned a stern gaze in Logan's direction. "All right now, you. I got a couple of things to say."

"Ruby—"

"No. Let me do the talking, 'cause we only got a minute. First thing, stop asking that poor girl nosy questions. She ain't done nothing wrong, and she has every right to keep her private business to herself. I won't have her pestered to death under my roof. If she wants to tell us something, she'll tell us. Understand?"

"I understand. But—"

"I'm not done. The second thing is, she's welcome to stay, but you're going to have to help out."

Logan's mind had been trailing after Charlotte, but at Ruby's words, he snapped to attention.

Ruby never asked for help.

"Are you feeling bad again?" Ruby had suffered a couple of what she called "sinking spells" over the summer. Her kids had been on high alert ever since.

"Nothing's wrong with me except old age, and there ain't no cure for that. Settle down. Aren't you and the rest of 'em always telling me that I shouldn't work myself so hard?"

"Yes." This was true. They'd been after Ruby for some time to slow down and take better care of herself. Not that she'd ever listened.

"I'm happy to have Charlotte here, but by end of day I get worn out. Fixing a big supper, cleaning up, all that's going to be hard on me. So, you'd best plan on coming by every evening after work to help. Think you can do that?"

"Sure." He studied his foster mother. He didn't know what was up, but something definitely was.

"Maybe you should take some time off work. I know you got that election coming up, but a few hours here and there shouldn't hurt your chances any. Besides, don't you have a bunch of vacation days you ain't used?"

"Yes." Of course he did. He never took vacation days.

"Good. And there's something else. The girl's pregnant and not feeling too good, by the look of her. I ain't comfortable having her here in her condition, not with me way out here all by my lonesome. What if she went into labor?"

Logan's concern ramped up a notch. "You heard what she said. She's not due for another couple months."

"Babies don't follow schedules, son. No, I'd feel better if you settled into the old cabin for a while. I ain't had time to find a new renter since Neil and Maggie bought their new house, so it's standing empty. I'll rest easier knowing you're just up the hill and close so you can get here quick if we have any problems."

None of this sounded like Ruby. "Are you *sure* you're feeling all right?"

She lifted an eyebrow. "I just need your help, son, with a visitor that you brought here with no warning. Don't that sound reasonable?"

Well, yeah. It did.

"Fine. I'll move to the cabin temporarily, and I'll spend my evenings over here helping out."

"And you'll take some time off. Once Charlotte gets to feeling better, she'll get tired of staying cooped up with an old lady, and she'll need some entertaining."

"I'll see what I can do. But I doubt Charlotte's going to feel like doing much. I brought her up here to rest. Besides, she hasn't been widowed all that long. She's probably still grieving."

"She needs to rest, for sure. But she's young. She'll bounce back quick." Ruby drew in a slow breath and shrugged. "As for the grieving, I got a feeling she'll come to the end of that quicker than most, if she hasn't already. All right. We've made ourselves a deal. Now why don't you bring in Charlotte's things so she can get herself settled in?"

"Okay, I'll see to it. And Ruby? Thanks."

She flapped a hand at him and smiled. "Get on with you."

Looking at his foster mom's kind, wrinkled face, Logan

felt the same surge of relief that he often felt after he'd
worked a bad wreck. In the thick of an emergency, he
moved fast, administering first aid, keeping folks calm,
and, most importantly, radioing for assistance. Only when
the injured had been loaded into the ambulances and were
speeding to the hospital would he relax, knowing he'd done
his best for them.

He'd done his best for Charlotte, too. She'd be well
looked after here. He and Ruby would see to that.

He gave his mom a quick, hard hug and headed out to
the truck for the suitcases.

Charlotte had lingered outside the kitchen door, listening to Ruby's and Logan's muffled voices and biting her
lip. When Ruby had fussed at him for asking questions,
followed by the words *she ain't done nothing wrong,* Charlotte stepped out of earshot, embarrassed.

Ruby might change her opinion if she caught her guest
eavesdropping. Living with Elizabeth—she and Dylan
had moved in with his mother shortly after they'd found
out about the baby—had nudged her into a lot of not-so-
great habits.

The truth was, over the past few months, listening outside closed doors had turned into a survival skill.

She walked down the short hallway, thinking. Logan's
questions worried her. He'd never liked unsolved puzzles,
and he'd always been good at figuring them out.

That might be a problem. She trusted Logan, but he'd
always had a straight-and-narrow way of looking at things.
If he found out just how bad her marriage had gotten, he
might stir up trouble.

And more trouble was the last thing she needed right
now.

What she did need was some peace and quiet to recover,

and thanks to Logan, she had that. She'd never imagined she'd be so grateful to come back to Cedar Ridge.

Charlotte had come to live with her grandparents at the age of twelve, when her mother had passed away. She'd mourned for her creative, fun-loving mom and the city life they'd both loved. She'd missed visiting museums and interesting restaurants, and she'd longed for opportunities to explore her love of fabrics and art.

This old-fashioned mountain town was sweet, but her interests and tastes had set her apart here. She'd been a little too artsy to click with most of the kids at school, and she'd had an inconvenient habit of speaking her thoughts out loud. Thanks to her grandparents' social status, she'd gotten along all right; she just hadn't had any really close friends.

Until she'd met Logan. He'd actually appreciated her tactless honesty, and he'd accepted her exactly the way she was.

He'd turned out to be the best friend she'd ever had in her life. And having him show up in her hospital room this morning, so solid and familiar, when everything in her life was going straight down the drain…she'd wanted to cling to his neck and cry like a baby.

Her faithful old friend and his spur-of-the-moment invitation were God's answers to her desperate prayers. She'd realized that, when they'd all clasped hands to say grace, and Ruby had mentioned being grateful for the folks brought to her table. Charlotte couldn't remember the last time she'd heard a blessing spoken over a meal—or when anybody had been thankful to have her nearby.

Yes, she believed God had brought her back here on purpose. This quiet farm was the perfect place for her to think and pray. Hopefully she'd be able to figure out some way to handle her mother-in-law and create a good life for her baby and for herself.

Charlotte opened the door of the room Ruby had suggested. She remembered it well. It had been the girls' room, crowded with three narrow beds and always littered with makeup, stuffed animals and discarded clothing.

It looked different now. A double bed with plenty of pillows was draped with a sensible navy coverlet, a thicker cream-colored blanket folded at its foot. A matching maple dresser, nightstand and bookcase stood sturdily in their places, and a big floral armchair with a footstool promised a wonderful spot for a nap.

The whole room was practical and pleasant, but it would've made Elizabeth's overpriced interior designer retch.

That fact only made Charlotte like it better. She crossed to the window and drew the curtain aside.

There was enough light to see the side yard and the path leading to the old cabin. Still-green leaves fluttered in the evening wind, and an owl was sounding off in the woods. Charlotte stood, cradling her curved belly with one hand and soaking in the peace of the farm until there was a knock on the door.

At her invitation, Logan came in, carrying the suitcases she'd packed when they'd stopped by Elizabeth's echoing house.

The cases were a silent reminder of a very uncomfortable twenty minutes. After being discharged from the hospital, Logan had driven her to the Tremaine home. She'd hurried to her beautifully appointed bedroom, tossing clothes and toiletries into her suitcases. Elizabeth had glowered icily in the doorway as if they might steal the silver if she took her eyes off them.

I'll be in touch, Elizabeth had said as they'd walked out the door. She'd made it sound like a threat.

Which, of course, it was.

"I think this is everything." Logan set both suitcases on the flat top of a hope chest. "I told Ruby you packed in a hurry, and she said to let her know if you forgot anything. She also said there were fresh towels in the bathroom if you want to get a shower." He glanced around the room. "This is a far cry from your big house in Savannah, I know, but you should be comfortable enough."

"It's perfect, and that wasn't my house. It belongs to Dylan's mother." And she planned to move out of it just as soon as she could scrape enough money together.

"You all right, honey?" Ruby poked her head in from the hallway. "Those sheets are good and fresh, washed and hung out on the line just a few days past. Now I got to get my goats settled for the night. Think you two could start on the supper dishes?"

"Of course!" Charlotte said, grateful for the distraction. Ruby smiled and headed toward the back door.

"I'll handle the cleanup," Logan said. "That doctor was pretty firm about you staying off your feet."

"I've been off my feet all day. I'm planning to make it an early night, but I'd like to help. It'll make me feel like I'm carrying my own weight. Which," she added, patting her rounded stomach, "is more of a job these days than it used to be."

Logan still looked uncertain, but he nodded. "If you say so."

Back in the kitchen, they started the homey process of wiping the dishes and filling Ruby's sink with soapy water.

"I haven't washed dishes by hand in ages." Charlotte trailed a finger through the feathery suds.

"You'll do plenty of it here. Ruby won't allow a dishwasher on the property. Ryder bought her one last Mother's Day, but she wouldn't let the truck driver unload it. They had a standoff right in the front yard."

Charlotte laughed and then froze, surprised at herself. How long had it been since she'd actually laughed?

A long time.

"You okay?" Logan dried one of Ruby's plain white plates with a red-checkered dishcloth. "You look like you had a twinge or something. Don't be shy about speaking up if you aren't feeling well. The doctor made it sound like you should be extra careful."

Charlotte darted a glance at him. "She's concerned. With…everything that's been going on…this pregnancy has been a little difficult."

"I imagine so." Logan finished wiping the plate and set it in a cupboard. "I'm sorry I missed Dylan's funeral, Charlotte. If I'd known, I'd have been there."

Charlotte kept her eyes on the platter she was washing. "That's okay."

She was thankful he hadn't come. Logan had a way of noticing things. He wouldn't have been fooled by the sunglasses she'd worn, hiding the black eye a drunken Dylan had given her when she'd tried to take his car keys that last night.

If Logan had known about that…

"Charlotte? You done with that platter?"

"Oh! Yes." She handed it over and started scrubbing a saucepan. "Sorry. I'm sure you're tired and ready to get home."

"I'm in no hurry. It takes me back, standing here, washing dishes. Ruby used to make us take turns." He smiled. "My day was Tuesday. The other kids complained, but I never minded so much. It made me feel more like a part of the family, having chores to do."

"Working alongside one another brings folks together. Always has." Ruby spoke from the doorway. Charlotte wasn't the only one listening to other people's conversations tonight. "My animals are all tucked in, so I'll take over in here. No, I'll have no arguments. This'll be your job starting tomorrow, but tonight you're both tuckered out. Besides, you still need to pack yourself a bag and drive back to the cabin, Logan. Did he tell you, Charlotte? He's staying there while you're visiting so he'll be close by if we need him."

"Oh, but I don't want to put you out," Charlotte protested.

"You're not. I like the cabin, and Ruby's right. Better if I'm close by, just in case that baby decides to come early."

"Go on." Ruby took the dish towel from her son and popped him on the rear with it. "Scat. Charlotte, you walk him out, will you? Make sure the front door shuts good. Sometimes that lock doesn't catch."

Logan frowned. "Since when?"

"Started a few weeks ago."

"You haven't mentioned it."

"I didn't want to bother you. Now, shoo."

Charlotte followed Logan through the house, watching as he absentmindedly used one foot to straighten a rumpled rug in the living room. After Dylan, it felt strange to be with a man like this, a man who liked washing dishes, and who straightened rugs and carried in other people's suitcases.

Outside, the cool evening air was wafting down from the mountains, and a choir of leftover summer frogs were singing lustily from the woods.

"I'll run to my apartment and bag up a few things. Then I'll be back at the cabin for the night. Here." Logan handed her a business card, emblazoned with a gold star.

"That has my number on it. Don't hesitate to call if you need anything. Okay?"

"I'm turning your life inside out, Logan. I'm sorry."

"This is what friends are for. To help each other out when things get hard." He hesitated. "I'm still your friend, Charlotte. Lots of things have changed over the years, but that never has, at least not for me. You know that, right?"

It took a minute for her to answer. "Always," she whispered around the lump in her throat.

"Always," he agreed softly, his eyes crinkling around the edges at the familiar word. "That means you can tell me anything. Ruby told me not to pry, and I won't. But if there's anything you need to talk about, I'm here."

She patted his forearm—it felt like patting a rock. Then she looked away, over the darkening farm, hoping he couldn't read her expression.

Because he was wrong. There were some things she couldn't tell him.

"Charlotte?"

She glanced at him and forced a smile. "Thanks, but I'm all right."

Even in the dim light, she could see he didn't quite believe her, but he nodded.

"Let me know if that changes. Okay?" He waited for her nod before walking down the porch steps.

Charlotte watched his taillights disappear down the mountain, rubbing her arms, even though the air wasn't really that chilly. In just a little while, she reminded herself, he'd be close by, in the log cabin just up the mountain path.

She found that idea so comforting that she wanted to cry.

But she didn't. Instead, she walked back inside and carefully checked the front door latch. It seemed perfectly fine to her. Then she went to argue with Ruby over which of them was going to sweep the kitchen floor.

Chapter Four

Charlotte woke to the clatter of dishes, and the smells of fresh bread and coffee. She glanced at the phone she'd set on the table by the bed, frowned and looked again.

She'd missed a call from Elizabeth, but she'd expected that. The surprise was that she'd only called once. Of course, she'd probably followed that up with a poisonously polite email.

No, it was the time showing on the screen that brought Charlotte up short. Half past nine.

She hadn't slept this late—or this well—in months. There was something so restful about this place. Last night as she'd snuggled down in the bed, she'd heard the old farmhouse creaking comfortably around her, heard Ruby's snores coming from the bedroom across the hall. She'd felt warm and safe and protected. And when she'd remembered that Logan was up at the cabin, the last of her tense muscles had relaxed, and she'd drifted effortlessly into sleep.

Leaving the phone on the nightstand, she padded barefoot to the old-fashioned bathroom before dressing in her favorite maternity smock and stretchy jeans. She automatically started pulling her hair into the smooth twist that Elizabeth had not-so-tactfully suggested years ago, but at the last minute, she tied it back in a defiant ponytail.

Then she followed her nose to the kitchen.

Ruby was pouring coffee into a chipped mug proclaiming World's Best Mom in glittery letters. She smiled as Charlotte came in.

"A good night's sleep's done its work. You look a sight better. Come in and sit down. I got breakfast all ready. Eggs, fruit and my homemade whole wheat bread."

As she spoke, Ruby placed the food on the table. Before Charlotte knew what had happened, she was biting into a slice of warm bread slathered with butter and blackberry jam.

Ruby settled across from her, mug in hand. "Glad to see you don't have morning sickness to deal with."

"Not anymore, thankfully." Charlotte took a bite of eggs—delicious, and with that rich golden color that only seemed to come from country hens. "This is wonderful."

"There's different kinds of jam. Blackberry's Logan's favorite, so I got it out for him, but I got strawberry, too, and a real good pear honey, if you'd like to try that."

Charlotte paused, a second forkful of eggs halfway to her mouth. "Logan was here?"

"Been and gone over an hour ago." Ruby had risen and was rummaging through her refrigerator, setting various mason jars of jam within her guest's reach.

"Why did he come by?"

"To check on you, of course. He waited as long as he could, hoping you'd wake up, but finally he had to get on to work." Ruby pulled spoons from a drawer and set them by the jams. "That was all right. He understood you needed your sleep." Ruby caught Charlotte looking at her. "You ain't surprised, are you? If you are, you've forgotten how that boy is. He'll be as pestery as a broody hen while you're here, you can count on that." Ruby settled back into her chair with a soft grunt. "That's one reason I told him to move to the cabin. It'll make it easier for him to see to you."

"I don't want him to feel like he has to look after me." Charlotte shifted uncomfortably in the ladder-back chair.

Ruby chuckled. "Nothing you can do about that. Logan looks after everybody. He brought you here, so the way he sees it, you're his responsibility." She lifted her mug for a sip.

"I'm my own responsibility," Charlotte corrected.

"Every pot's got to rest on its own bottom, that's true. It's also true that we all need help sometimes. I'd say you need a fair bit right now, especially with that little one coming."

Charlotte glanced down at her rounded middle, unsure how to answer.

The older woman smiled. "Logan's bossy self and this old farm are the good Lord's special provision for you, I think. You feel that yourself, deep down, and that's why you came along home with him. It's an instinct, like a wounded animal heading for the safest place it knows, and like most God-given instincts, it's a good one. You'll be all right here while you sort yourself out. And don't worry, I won't ask any nosy questions. Don't need to. I already got a good idea of what's been going on."

Charlotte lifted her head, searching the older woman's eyes. The expression on Ruby's face remained calm and unbothered.

"Do you?"

"Honey, I've been around a long time. When a sweet-hearted pregnant widow like you ain't grieving hard for the young husband she lost—and you're not, don't bother denying that—and she shies at quick moves and keeps her eyes cast down, well…" Ruby set her lips together. "I can figure out what that means. What was it that turned him mean? Drink?"

There didn't seem to be much point in denying it, so Charlotte nodded.

"It'll do that." Sympathy glimmered in Ruby's eyes. "And it's always a shame when it does. But it's all over now, and we won't talk about it anymore unless you want to."

"Don't tell Logan."

"Not my business to tell, but secrets don't stand much chance around that boy. He's likely to figure things out for himself, and it might be better if he heard it from you. But that's your choice, not mine. Now, let's talk about something else. You given any thought to how you plan to put in your time while you're here?"

Charlotte breathed a sigh of relief. This seemed like a much safer subject. "No, but if there's anything I can do to help out—"

"Not much, I don't reckon. Logan's made it plenty clear that you're to stay off your feet as much as possible. But I was thinking about something you could do sitting down. Just so you don't get too bored." The older woman spoke almost shyly, and that caught Charlotte's attention.

When had outspoken Ruby Sawyer ever acted shy? Whatever this was about, it must be important to her.

Charlotte added a spoonful of blackberry jam to her last bite of bread. "Absolutely, Ruby. What do you have in mind?"

"Well, seeing how you're so handy with your needle, I thought you could help me with a project."

"I'd be happy to. What is it?"

"It's like this. You know all my kids came to me from hard places, and most of the time they barely brought anything with them. A few clothes in a trash bag, maybe, but not much else."

Charlotte nodded. She'd known Logan had been a foster child. He'd come to Ruby's home as a young teenager, and she'd gathered the past he'd left behind had been a rough one. He'd never talked much about it, and after a few unsuccessful attempts to get him to, she'd left it alone.

"Being uprooted like that is real hard on kids," Ruby went on. "All my young'uns hung on to stuff, 'cause they had so little they could keep. So about a week ago my Maggie—you remember her, don't you?"

"Of course."

"She got married a while back, and she just had a baby daughter. She told me she's saving all Gracie's outgrown clothes with the idea of making her a memory quilt, something she can pass down to her own child one day. Maggie said it bothered her that she didn't have any of her adopted son Oliver's baby clothes, but she decided she'd just make him one out of the clothes he's outgrowing now."

"That's a nice idea."

"Ain't it? But I realized that Maggie doesn't have anything like that her own self." Ruby shook her head. "None of my kids do. It's been weighing on my mind. But then, I remembered the old clothes I stored up in the attic, and I thought maybe I could make one, after all."

"You want to make Maggie a memory quilt?"

"I want to make one for each of my kids. There's six of them, you know, so that'll take a while. Here's my problem—I don't have the foggiest notion how to start. I can sew on a button just fine, and even hem up clothes pretty good. But a quilt," the older woman shrugged, "especially one made from scraps, now that's a bit of a reach."

Charlotte's interest was piqued. "A project like that does have some challenges. It's different, working with salvaged fabrics. Nowadays, most quilts are made with new materials, but traditionally, they were made just like what you're talking about, from worn-out odds and ends. Different fabrics will handle differently, so you'll have to use some thought in how you combine them. Also, there'll be the problem of the design itself, arranging the available colors and patterns in a way that looks good."

"And I'd like the quilts to be just like my kids," Ruby hurried to add. "You know, each one different."

"You want custom designs." Charlotte's mind ticked over what she knew about Logan's foster sister. Maggie was kindhearted, always baking treats for her family and friends. Her cookies had been legendary in high school, and Charlotte hadn't been surprised to hear that the friendly girl was now part owner of Angelo's, Cedar Ridge's beloved bakery.

Yes, with a little thought, she could come up with the perfect quilt for Maggie.

"That's right," Ruby said. "So? You willing to help? Just with the first quilt," she hastened to add. "Once you get me started, I can muddle on by myself for the rest of 'em."

"I'd love to help you." Charlotte had looked forward to taking a break from sewing, but she meant what she was saying.

After years of fussing with silk, satin, pearl buttons and lace, she relished the idea of tackling a simple old-fashioned quilt. And an authentic one, made from scraps, designed for somebody she truly liked?

That sounded like fun.

"Great!" Ruby rose and dragged two large plastic bins over from the corner. "I was hoping you'd say that, so I asked Logan to haul these down from the attic. I ain't so good at carrying stuff up and down stairs anymore." She unsnapped the top. "Let's see what we got to work with."

Charlotte pulled out several shirts, her mind shifting into creative mode as she noted patterns and colors. Then she frowned, riffling through the clothing until she reached the bottom of the container. She opened the second tote, rummaged through its contents, then sat back and sighed.

It was ridiculous how disappointed she felt.

"These are the wrong bins, Ruby. They're full of boys' clothes. I'd carry down the ones with Maggie's stuff for you, but—" she gestured at her rounded tummy "—that's probably not a good idea. When Logan comes back, maybe he can find the right ones. In the meantime, if you'll give me some paper and a pencil, I'll sketch some ideas for Maggie's quilt."

The older woman shook her head. "We've had a misunderstanding, honey. Maggie put the idea in my head, but I figured on starting with Logan's quilt. He's the oldest, and besides he's the one you know the best."

"Oh!" Charlotte looked down at the jumbled shirts, and her eye lit on a familiar forest green one.

Yes, these were Logan's. She remembered this one. It had been his favorite for a while in high school, and he'd worn it almost every other day. That had been their junior year, when he'd first started wearing that cedar-scented aftershave. She'd teased that people were going to start mistaking him for a tree.

She pulled out the shirt and lifted it to her nose. Even after all these years, she thought she detected a whiff of cedar.

Ruby cleared her throat, and Charlotte glanced up, the shirt crumpled against her face. Embarrassed, she lowered it.

"These should be washed," she said, flustered. "It's best to work with clean fabric."

Ruby lifted one eyebrow, but she nodded. "I'll tend

to that while you draw out the pattern. I'm sure you can think of one, seeing as how you and Logan were such good friends."

She already had. Maggie's pattern would've taken some time, but Charlotte had known immediately what kind of quilt she'd create for Logan. It had come to her easily, instantly, not like the bridal dresses she often struggled with. She could *see* this quilt, the way she used to see her designs in her head back before—

Back before.

"Bring me that paper, Ruby," she said. "I know just the thing."

Logan navigated the curves of Ruby's winding drive, steadying the overstuffed sack of groceries in the passenger seat of his patrol car with his free hand. He'd called Maggie to ask what pregnant women should eat, and she'd told him—eventually. She'd demanded an explanation first.

"I knew it," his sister had crowed. "Ruby's determined to see us all married before she 'goes to glory,' as she puts it. You're next up on her to-do list, and she's picked out Charlotte. Smart. Since you had that big crush on her back in school, Ruby's halfway to the finish line already."

He'd protested, not that it had done any good. This was a familiar argument. Maggie had teased him about Charlotte all through high school, claiming there was more than friendship going on between the two of them—at least on his end.

There hadn't been. Logan parked and reached across the seat to grab the groceries. Sure, he liked Charlotte—he had since the day she'd plopped herself down at his lunch table. But what he'd felt for her had never been one of those up-and-down, kick-to-the-gut romantic crushes. His feelings had gone way deeper and lasted a lot longer.

Maybe he'd had the occasional moment where his feelings had drifted sideways a little. That was normal—healthy even, for a guy spending so much time with an attractive girl. But he'd never let those thoughts go anywhere. He and Charlotte had been best friends, and he wasn't about to let some temporary romantic silliness ruin that.

He walked to the porch, trying to keep the yogurt from tumbling out of the sack and thinking about Charlotte. Her honesty had drawn him first. His father was a professional liar, and Logan had learned to hate dishonesty. She was the first girl he'd ever met who told him the absolute truth, and he'd appreciated that.

He'd also come to admire her kindness. The whole time he'd known her, she'd habitually gone out of her way to befriend people other folks overlooked.

Like him.

But not only him. Charlotte had found some quality to like about every outcast in the school. That got her into messes sometimes, and he'd warned her to be more cautious—not that she'd ever listened. As a result, he'd spent a significant amount of time pushing himself between Charlotte and trouble, but he couldn't stay irritated with her.

She was just so…likable, and she had a knack for making him laugh. She was naturally a happy person herself, and she shared joy as easily as she shared chewing gum.

He hadn't seen much joy back in that Savannah hospital room, though. It had hit him hard, seeing her lying there so pale, without the old sparkle in her eyes. It made him mad, too, and he'd wanted to do something. He'd wanted to *fix* it.

So he'd brought her home, to Cedar Ridge and to Ruby. As long as Charlotte was here, he could see to it that nobody bothered her, that she was looked after, fed plenty of yogurt and fruit and all that other healthy stuff Maggie had told him to buy. He could give her a chance to find her balance, get that old sparkle back, maybe.

If people wanted to think he had some sort of leftover schoolboy crush on her, fine. Let them.

He didn't bother knocking. None of them ever did. Wherever Ruby was, her kids were always welcome.

He did stop to inspect the door latch, though. Just as he'd suspected, the thing worked fine. He could almost hear Maggie snickering.

He was halfway through the living room when he heard voices coming from the kitchen.

"I think these three yellow ones," Charlotte was saying, "and that blue one, maybe. Unless we want to warm it up. Then we should use this light red button-up. It's pretty faded, but it's a nice color."

"I remember that shirt." Ruby's chuckle drifted through the closed door. "I warned him the color wouldn't hold. Sure enough, it ran the first time he washed it. He wore pink boxers for two weeks before he admitted it and let me bleach them out. That's a memory, for sure. Let's stick it in."

That story sounded suspiciously familiar. Logan juggled the groceries so that he could turn the battered metal doorknob.

Ruby and Charlotte were barely visible behind a kitchen table mounded with piles of his old shirts, from the bins he'd assumed were bound for the local thrift store. The two women looked up and smiled.

"Hi," Charlotte said. Was he imagining it, or did she look a little brighter today?

"What are you doing?"

"Sewing. Or getting ready to." Charlotte nudged one

stack of clothing to the side. "We've got everything we need from the bins, Ruby. Should Logan carry them back upstairs for you?"

"No point. If you've got all you need, I'll donate the rest. What do you have there, son?" Ruby nodded toward the sack he'd put on the counter.

"I picked up groceries." As Ruby rose to rummage through the bag, he asked, "What kind of sewing?"

"It's your mom's idea. She should tell you." Charlotte continued folding shirts with quick, sure movements.

As Ruby explained about something called a memory quilt, he grew more and more confused—and suspicious. His foster mom had never shown any interest in sewing before. She was always impatient with inside work, preferring to putter with her garden and her animals. Now she'd suddenly taken up quilting just when Charlotte came to visit? Using *his* old clothes—most of which dated back from high school, the years he'd spent with Charlotte.

Maybe Maggie wasn't so far off.

When Charlotte left the room for a minute, he shot his foster mom a hard look. "Since when do you like to sew?"

"I don't." Ruby was stowing items in her fridge. "Charlotte does, and she's the one who counts. She needs something to keep her hands and her mind busy. Son, this sure is a lot of yogurt!"

"Maggie said to get plenty. Why'd you start with my quilt?"

"Because Charlotte knows you best. This is a good idea, Logan. Don't start fussing and spoil it."

Before he could answer, Charlotte opened the door. "I have the color scheme worked out, Ruby, but we'll need material for the border and the backing. We should order that so we're sure to get enough. I know just the place.

They sell quality material and ship fast. Do you have a computer? I could go ahead and place the order."

Ruby shook her head. "I don't have internet here."

Logan turned to look at her. "Yes, you do. Ryder and I had it hooked up two months ago."

"I canceled it. Folks want to get in touch with me, they can do it the old-fashioned way. Write me a nice letter or call me on the phone. Or better yet, come out here and sit on the porch awhile."

"Ruby—"

"The cabin's got internet. You could drive Charlotte over there while I get supper started, couldn't you?"

Logan studied her. He smelled a setup. "I could do that, yeah."

"Great." Ruby beamed. "Supper'll take a while, so don't feel like you have to rush back."

He looked at Charlotte, who shrugged. "I'd like to get the fabric ordered, if it's not too much trouble. I'm excited about this."

Maybe she was. She sure looked more like herself. Her hair was up in a messy ponytail, and little curls had fallen loose to frame her face. There was even a smudge of pink on her cheeks.

This quilt idea of Ruby's was helping. That was all he needed to know.

"No trouble at all. Let's go."

He shepherded Charlotte out of the kitchen and settled her in the front seat of the patrol car. As they headed down the driveway she looked around with interest.

"I'm glad I get to ride in the front. Do you like being sheriff?"

"I do." He darted a glance at her. "Wasn't sure I would. Being sheriff means more paperwork and more politics, and those have never been my favorite things."

"Why'd you run, then? If you weren't sure?"

"It seemed the right thing to do at the time."

Charlotte leaned back in her seat, considering him. "Ruby says you ran because you like taking care of people."

So they'd been talking about him. He wasn't sure how he felt about that. "My sister Torey says it's because I like ordering people around."

Charlotte laughed. "She might have something there."

He followed the fork leading to the cabin. The drive hadn't been maintained as well since Maggie and Neil moved, and he winced as the car bumped up the rutted path.

Once Charlotte sucked in a breath, but when he looked at her, she shook her head. "Just a kick. Sometimes he surprises me."

He glanced at the roundness in her middle. "It's a boy?"

"Yes."

"Maggie's is a girl. Cutest thing you ever saw. They named her Gracie, but I call her Gingersnap."

Charlotte smiled. "Because she's red-headed like Maggie?"

"Because Maggie was baking gingersnaps when she went into labor and wouldn't leave for the hospital until the last batch was out of the oven. Neil nearly had a heart attack." Logan recalled the healthy glow Maggie'd had throughout her pregnancy, so different from Charlotte.

"Look," he said, stopping in front of the cabin. "Don't overdo with this quilt, okay? You're supposed to be resting."

"Helping Ruby with the quilt will be fun. Don't worry."

Easier said than done. "Hold up. The ground up here's rocky. I'll walk with you."

She sighed, but she waited, looping her arm through his

as they went across the yard and onto the porch. While he unlatched the door, she surveyed the panorama of sloping forest, highlighted by the slanting afternoon sunshine. "This must feel like living in a tree house. If I were you, I'd stay up here all the time."

"It is nice." He motioned her inside and flipped on the lights. "A lot bigger than my apartment and quieter, too. But I work pretty much all the time, so I'm hardly ever home anyway." He tapped keys on the laptop he'd left open on the desk. "Here you go," he said. "Order away."

Charlotte lowered herself into the chair, and soon her fingers were flying over the keyboard. "This won't take long. I know exactly what I want." Within seconds, she was studying a screen of fabrics, her lips pursed in a pout of concentration.

"Take your time." He'd better make sure the bathroom was safe for humanity. When Maggie had been expecting, she'd known the quickest route to every restroom in town.

He tidied the bathroom, wiping the sink clean and making sure everything was female friendly. When he stepped back into the living room, Charlotte was still absorbed in the computer—but she wasn't looking at fabric. She'd opened an email program, probably taking the opportunity to check her inbox. She was frowning and biting her lip as she read.

He shut the bathroom door, and Charlotte jumped as if she'd heard a gunshot. She quickly exited the program and shut the laptop.

"All done." Her voice shook a little.

"You sure? If there's anything else you need to see about online, go ahead. We're in no hurry."

"No." Charlotte stood. "I'm ready to go. The fabric should be delivered in a few days."

"Ruby will be happy."

He wasn't happy, though. He was concerned.

In all the years he'd known her, Charlotte had never once jumped when he'd walked into a room, and she'd never hidden anything from him, either. He'd seen other women jerk like that, though, plenty of times. That quick, defensive movement reminded him of the wives he dealt with on domestic calls—women who had to stay alert and conceal things just to survive.

He'd noticed some signs like that in the hospital, too, and he didn't like the picture he was piecing together. Something must have gone very wrong in Charlotte's marriage, and he wasn't sure she trusted him enough to tell him about it.

But that didn't mean he couldn't find out.

Chapter Five

Two nights later, Charlotte hung the damp dish towel on its hook over Ruby's kitchen sink while Logan stowed the final pots and pans in their appointed cupboards.

They'd just finished cleaning the kitchen together. Even though she hadn't been here long, she'd already eased into a soothing routine. Days spent sewing with Ruby, supper with Logan and Ruby and then cleanup duty.

Except for the cell phone buzzing angrily every so often, everything had been peaceful. She'd felt a little guilty blowing off her mother-in-law's calls, but after reading Elizabeth's nastygram of an email, she had even less desire to answer the phone. She'd justified it by remembering what Dr. Edwards had said about eliminating stress. Dealing with Dylan's mother was the definition of stress.

So, this morning, after sending a short text letting Elizabeth know that all was well, Charlotte had stowed the phone in the bedside table drawer.

Under a nice, thick towel.

She'd better enjoy this break because it wouldn't last long. Dylan's mother had a talent for making herself heard—and for getting her way.

Charlotte sighed and rubbed her baby bump.

"You all right?"

She looked up to find Logan studying her. He didn't miss much. Probably a good thing in a law enforcement officer, but it was startling sometimes.

"I'm fine," she said brightly. "Or I would be if I hadn't had that second helping of cheese potatoes."

"You're eating for two," Logan pointed out. "If your stomach's upset, want me to fix you a cup of peppermint tea? You said it helped before."

She *had* mentioned that, casually. So tonight he'd arrived bearing two boxes of peppermint tea, different brands because he wasn't sure which kind was her favorite.

She'd stood there, a box in each hand, blinking back silly tears as she struggled for the right words to say. It was just such a thoughtful gesture, and it had been so long since anybody had done something like that for her, something sweet and simple and kind.

She'd finally mumbled an awkward thanks, which he'd waved off with a no-big-deal smile. But it was a big deal to her, and whenever she looked at the boxes stacked on the counter, her heart did a grateful flip.

"I'm all right," she said now. "I should be chipping in on the groceries, though. I'm sure Ruby's on a fixed income, and I'm getting expensive to feed."

Logan glanced sideways at her and grinned. "I wouldn't suggest that to Ruby, if I were you. She considers feeding people part of her mission in life. Besides, there's no need to worry. Between the six of us kids, we see that her pantry's stuffed full."

She was sure they did. "It's not your job to feed me either."

"It is for now," Logan stated. "You're our guest. Anyhow, you're earning your keep with that sewing project

Ruby's started, the one with my old shirts. When do I get to see that, by the way?"

"When it's done. Ruby wants it to be a surprise." She smiled. "So you'd better stop trying to sneak in and catch us working on it."

"Noticed that, did you?" Logan's grin widened. "You'll also notice it didn't do me a bit of good. Ruby's got ears like a bat."

"I had to have good ears." Ruby came in, shutting the kitchen door behind herself. "Otherwise, no telling what you six might have gotten up to when my back was turned." She surveyed the cleaned kitchen with a smile. "You two have done a bang-up job. Now, Logan, why don't you take our Charlotte for a turn around the meadow? It's a beautiful evening, and she could do with a walk. Yes," she added with a twinkle in her eyes, "I saw how many of my potatoes you ate. Nothing wrong with that, but you want to balance it out with some exercise."

"You coming, too?" Logan cast a sharp look at Ruby, who flapped an age-spotted hand.

"I'm feeling a little tired. I think I'll sit myself down and read awhile. You two go enjoy the last of the sunshine."

The older woman slipped back through the door and disappeared down the hallway. Logan watched her go then turned to Charlotte. "So? Feel like taking a walk?"

"Oh, you don't have to. You must be tired after working all day." He was still wearing his sheriff's uniform, which meant he hadn't even taken time to stop by the cabin to change.

"A walk will do him good, same as you." Ruby's voice drifted up the hall. "He ate plenty of them potatoes, too."

Logan laughed. "Sounds like it's settled." He walked to the door and held it open. "Ready?"

"Well." Charlotte hesitated. A walk was probably a good

idea. Dr. Edwards had encouraged gentle daily exercise, and sewing required a lot of sitting. "All right."

They made it down the steps and had started toward the rear of the property when Ruby rapped on the window.

"Take her arm, son! Don't want her catching her foot in some hole and taking a tumble. Not in her condition."

Logan winked and offered his arm. When Charlotte hesitated, there was another series of sharp knocks.

"You're going to get me in trouble," Logan teased.

So, Charlotte took his arm.

When she curved her fingers around his muscled forearm, her stomach did a trembly little dance, and the baby shifted position gently. It felt...weird, walking through the trim barnyard toward the back pasture arm in arm with Logan.

It shouldn't. He was just an old friend—a good one— and a kind and generous man.

But he was also so...tall. And walking alongside her in his uniform, he exuded an authority that comforted her and made her nervous all at the same time.

He led her past the barn and opened a wooden gate, weathered gray over the years. Charlotte had been watching her feet because Ruby was right—there were plenty of dips and holes. But when Logan paused to fasten the gate behind them, she looked up and caught a quick breath.

The late afternoon sun was slanting through the pines and across the small clearing in wide, lazy, golden stripes. The grass was about midcalf high and threaded with wildflowers. Tiny blooms of yellow, purple and dark blue were scattered through the waving grass like paint splattered playfully across an easel.

She normally worked in fabric nowadays, but the artist in Charlotte itched for a sketchpad. Pastels, she thought. She needed pastels for this, good ones, like the ones she bought at that art store down from the college. Watercolors would be too pale, colored pencils too precise.

Pastels that she could smudge and dot across a textured paper—that would come the closest to capturing this fresh loveliness.

"Are you all right?"

Logan was watching her. He'd turned his head against the sun, so his face was shadowed, but she could feel the sharpness of his eyes, checking her over.

"Yes. It's just so beautiful."

He looked back across the small pasture. "It is right now. We'll turn the goats and the donkey in here later, let 'em eat it down. But Ruby likes the flowers while they last, so we leave it alone until the first of October, usually. Come along by the fence. I cleared a strip here not long ago, just to make sure nothing needed fixing. It'll make for easier walking."

Charlotte breathed in deeply as they crossed the field. "It smells as pretty as it looks," she said. "I'd forgotten how fresh and clean the air is up here, and how cool and soft it feels. So much nicer than Savannah."

"Never thought I'd hear you say that. You couldn't wait to get to Savannah after high school."

"I wanted to learn about art," Charlotte answered absently, her eyes taking in the play of light over the golden broomsedge. "Savannah's the perfect place for that."

"Were you happy there?"

The question was gentle, casual, but a prickle of warning skittered across her shoulders. Years spent dealing with Tremaines had taught her to watch for minefields hidden in questions. Logan was probing.

"Yes, I was." That was true enough. She'd been happy for a while.

"You don't want to go back, though." He stopped to toss away a branch that had fallen over the fence. "Why's that?"

Charlotte kept her answer simple and honest. "Too many unhappy memories."

"Yeah, I guess there would be." He'd think she meant the ordinary sort of sad memories, the kind any widow would have. She didn't correct him. "I don't imagine that mother-in-law of yours is much of a draw, either."

It wasn't phrased as a question, but it was one. She hesitated.

One of the rules that had been stressed to her over and over again since she'd married Dylan was that you never criticized the family. Ever. Honesty wasn't appreciated and usually resulted in disaster.

She set her jaw. She was ready to stop taking orders from the Tremaines. Might as well start now.

"No," she said. "She isn't. Elizabeth can be very pushy. She likes everybody to fall in with her plans, and we've butted heads more than once."

Charlotte had won very few of those battles. That was another thing that was going to have to change, if she didn't want Elizabeth turning her grandson into a miniature version of Dylan.

Logan stopped walking, and she looked up at him curiously. He glanced at her, then stared off into the woods and heaved a sigh. "Speaking of people who like you to fall in with their plans, I'd better clue you in on something."

"What?"

"This is embarrassing, but I think Ruby's come up with a plan of her own. She's got some notion of you and me... ending up together."

Charlotte frowned. "Ending up together?"

Logan's jawline flushed a brick red. "Like...romantically."

"Oh!"

"She never married herself—probably never found a man who could keep up with her—but she's developed a weakness for matchmaking in her old age. She's determined to see all us kids married off, and when Maggie found a husband it only encouraged her. Apparently, I'm next on the list, and she's lit on you as the likeliest candidate. Sorry," he added sheepishly.

Charlotte couldn't help it. She laughed. "I guess it would be efficient anyway." She gestured toward her round middle. "Ready-made family."

Logan laughed, too, and he looked relieved. "Yeah. She could tick two things off her list if she matched us up. Anyway, I just wanted you to know—and to understand that I've got nothing to do with it. Ruby can get pretty heavy-handed with her hints. I didn't want you to feel uncomfortable."

She patted his arm. "You're talking to a very pregnant lady. Uncomfortable is my middle name. Don't worry. Ruby won't bother me. I know you've never looked at me that way." When Logan didn't answer, Charlotte clarified. "Romantically, I mean."

Logan started walking again. "Watch your step," he cautioned. "The light's going, and it's hard to see the ground under all this grass. You don't want to trip."

It wasn't much dimmer now than it had been a few minutes ago. Charlotte studied Logan's face. "You haven't, ever, have you? Looked at me that way?" When he stayed silent, she frowned. "I mean, we've always just been really good friends. Right?"

He sighed and stopped again. Leaning one elbow on the top of a weathered fence post, he looked away from her, toward the red-and-golden clouds celebrating the sunset.

"Mostly," he said finally. "Mostly I've thought of you as a friend."

"Mostly?"

There were times when Logan's commitment to absolute honesty was downright inconvenient. This was one of them.

Since she'd asked him a direct question, though, his only other option was to lie to her. For him, that was the same as not having any options at all.

"I was a sixteen-year-old guy hanging out with one of the prettiest girls in school. So sure, sometimes, my mind might've drifted in a romantic direction."

"Seriously?"

"What's serious when you're sixteen?" He tried to make a joke out of it because she was staring wide-eyed at him. "Come on, Charlotte. Cut me some slack. We were together all the time. You're telling me you never wondered what it would've been like if we'd started dating?"

He had, off and on. When one of his friends had a new girl and was all gooey in love. Or when Maggie or Torey or one of the others teased him about Charlotte, insisting that down deep he liked her more than he thought he did. Sure, he'd thought about it then.

Of course, sometimes the idea would hit him out of the blue—like when Charlotte had looked up at him a certain way, with friendly laughter sparkling in her eyes and her lips curved into a teasing smile.

Yeah. Especially then.

"No." Charlotte shook her head. "I didn't think about you that way."

"Ouch."

She swatted him. "It's not that. I always knew you were good-looking and smart and all those other things.

But…" Charlotte made a helpless gesture. "You were so much more than just another cute guy to me. We were best friends, Logan. I could talk to you about anything. I *did* talk to you about anything." She looked embarrassed. "And all that time you were thinking about…wondering…"

"Not *all* the time." This was excruciating. "Now and then, I said."

"I had no idea."

"Yeah, I can tell. Could we possibly change the subject? It was a long time ago, and it doesn't matter now, anyway. Water under the bridge."

"Okay. Sure." She nodded, but her eyes slipped south and landed on his lips. They lingered there, just for a few seconds before she looked away.

And he realized something, something that socked him so hard in his stomach he couldn't breathe for a second or two.

Maybe Charlotte had never thought about dating him back when they were in high school together, but she was thinking about it now.

Her eyes flitted back up to his, full of uncertainty and something else that he struggled to read. Regret? He wasn't sure, and before he could figure it out, the radio clipped on his left shoulder squawked.

"Roane County, 101?"

His call number. "Excuse me." He turned to the side and responded, "101."

"We've had a call from that location you're monitoring."

There was only one address in town that he'd requested to be notified about, no matter the hour. His mouth tightened.

"Dispatch, I'm 10-8 to that location," he said shortly. Then he turned back to Charlotte.

"You have to go," she said before he could.

"Yeah." He sighed. "Afraid so."

"Nothing dangerous, I hope."

She hadn't actually asked him a question, so technically he didn't have to answer, but she looked worried. "Just a domestic situation."

He'd thought that little sidestep would reassure her, but instead her hand tightened on his arm.

"Oh, no." Her brow creased. "Those can be…really bad sometimes."

They could be. "I've dealt with these people before." Numerous times. "It'll be all right. Come on. I'd better walk you back to the house."

She went silent as they picked their way across the field. The whip-poor-will was singing one of his last summer songs somewhere in the woods, and the breeze rippled through the tall grass making the flowers bob and sway.

When they'd first walked out into the field, Charlotte's face had lit up with joy. Now she seemed drained and worried, and she wasn't even looking at the pretty things around them.

He cast concerned glances down at her. Her brow was puckered, and she kept her free hand cupped over her belly. Protectively. Defensively.

Logan clamped his jaw down hard. Most citizens underestimated the danger in domestic calls, assuming that officers were more likely to get hurt responding to robberies or other violent crimes.

They were wrong. Logan had only had three officers injured over the past four years, and all three had occurred on domestic calls. Two of them had happened at this particular location, which was why he'd made it clear he would be the one responding there in future.

Charlotte clearly understood how dangerous this call

could be, and that was another piece of this puzzle clicking into place.

He didn't like the picture that was forming. Not one bit.

They'd reached the back porch of the farmhouse.

She looked up at him. "Thanks for walking with me."

"My pleasure."

"I'll see you tomorrow at suppertime." She reached up and gently straightened the badge on his chest. "Logan? You be careful. Please? Be really, really careful."

He frowned. Her hand was trembling. She was genuinely afraid for him.

"I will be." He caught her eye. "I promise you."

She bit her lip and managed a smile. "And you always tell the truth."

"Always." He stressed the word gently. "Charlotte?"

She'd turned toward the steps, but she stopped and looked over her shoulder. "What?"

Did Dylan hit you?

She wouldn't lie to him. He knew that. But he had to go to work and cope with a man who beat up his wife and son whenever he got a few swigs of liquor in his stomach. There wasn't time to get into Charlotte's story now, no matter how much he'd like to. It would have to wait.

But not for long.

"I'll see you soon," he said.

Chapter Six

It had been a tough night.

Logan pulled up in front of the darkened cabin and switched off the engine. He took a minute to massage his aching forehead before reaching up to click the button on his radio.

"101, Roane County. I'm 10-7, 10-42." Out of service, off duty.

For now, anyway.

"10-4, 101."

The night dispatcher sounded as tired as he felt. It was well past two o'clock in the morning, and the entire sheriff's office had spent the last several hours dealing with Albie Wilson, one of their most troublesome frequent fliers.

Not that it would do any good. Albie was cooling his heels in the drunk tank tonight, but he'd almost surely be released in the morning. Sherrie Wilson was too afraid of her husband to press charges. Logan had tried talking to her—again—but he had no reason to believe she'd be any more cooperative than she had been in the past.

That was too bad, because Logan was getting seriously worried about their son. Zeb had just hit fourteen, and tonight Logan had noticed a new, dangerous glint in the boy's eye as he watched his drunken father being wrestled into the patrol car.

Logan recognized that look all too well. He'd seen it on the faces of numerous boys, boys with dads like Albie or without any fathers in the picture at all.

He'd seen it in the mirror a few times, too, years ago.

It wasn't good news, that look, and it was one reason he was pushing to get a mentoring program off the ground, matching his deputies up with local boys who needed good male role models. An after-school mentor was no substitute for having a loving father in the home, but it was better than doing nothing while boys in his town floundered into trouble.

The program was supposed to get rolling in a few months, assuming he won the election as predicted. But after what he'd seen tonight, he had a sinking feeling it would come too late for Zeb.

Logan sighed and got out of the car.

At least up here, things were peaceful. The wind had settled, and the moonlit forest surrounding the cabin was silent. Whatever wild things were prowling tonight had ducked for cover when he'd driven up. Once he disappeared into the house, the usual nighttime rustlings would probably start up again.

Things always did seem to start up again, the minute his back was turned. It was frustrating, but that was the way the world worked.

He unlocked the door and tossed his keys onto the table. At the noise, something moved in the living room, and he heard a soft sigh.

Logan tensed, his gaze zeroing in on the form sleeping on the leather sofa, silvered over with the moonlight streaming through the cabin windows.

He stared, stunned. Charlotte. What was she doing here?

He edged sideways to get a better look. She seemed okay. She was stretched out on the couch, a blanket tucked around her round middle. One arm was curved under her cheek, and she had something gripped in her hand. He leaned forward and frowned. That was the T-shirt he'd worn yesterday. She was clutching it, crumpled against her face.

He didn't know why she'd pulled that out of his laundry basket, much less why she was sleeping with it. All he knew was that seeing her holding it was making his heart do funny things.

He pulled himself away long enough to do a quick check of the house. It proved to be empty. Ruby hadn't come with her, then.

Returning to the sofa, he frowned down at her. He could think of no reason why she'd be here. There was no car outside, so she'd either walked or been driven over. And why?

Only one way to find out. He tapped her shoulder.

At his touch, she jolted awake with a gasp, scrambling upright on the sofa.

"It's okay. It's just me." He snapped on the lamp.

"Logan!" She blinked and squinted in the light, rubbing at her eyes. Her face relaxed into relief. "You're back. What time is it?"

"Late." He dropped into the recliner and leaned forward, studying her. She looked a little dazed, but other than that he saw nothing obviously wrong. "Charlotte, what are you doing here?"

The relief ebbed into guilt, and she nudged his wrinkled T-shirt behind her. "Waiting on you."

"Why?"

"I was worried. I know it was silly, but…" she trailed off.

"Does Ruby know where you are?"

"She drove me here." Charlotte glanced at the clock and winced. "Hours ago. I was supposed to call her so she could come get me once you'd gotten home safe, but it's so late now. She probably fell asleep." She glanced at Logan. "We didn't think you'd be out so late. Ruby said it probably wouldn't take too long."

"The call took longer than I expected. That happens a lot. Ruby knows that. She should have warned you."

Three guesses why she hadn't. He was going to have to have a few stern words with his mother about this silly matchmaking stuff.

Charlotte must have read his expression. "Don't blame Ruby. This is my fault. After you left, I had a…little panic attack." She looked embarrassed. "Your mom could see I wasn't going to settle down until I knew you were home safe, so she suggested I come over and wait for you. Like I said, it was silly."

"No, not silly." Things were clicking into place. "I'm surprised Ruby left you here by yourself, though."

"She didn't want to. She waited with me for a couple hours, but I could see she was getting sleepy, so I made her go home."

Nobody ever *made* Ruby do anything, but he let that slide.

"I'm sorry I was so much trouble," Charlotte went on miserably. "I figured it must have been something really bad for them to call you back into work, and the more I thought about it… I'm sorry," she repeated.

"It's okay. But just so you know, I'm a small-town sheriff, so I'm never really off duty. And there are some situations I prefer to handle myself. That's all. I'm sorry it upset you."

"Not your fault." She attempted a smile. "It's probably

the pregnancy hormones. They get your emotions all in a twist."

"Maggie cried over detergent commercials for five months, I remember." He rubbed his chin. "Charlotte, I don't like secrets all that much."

"Logan—"

"Let me finish, okay? The way I see it, secrets are first cousins to lies, even when they're kept with the best intentions." He didn't have to explain how much he hated lies. She already knew. "Honesty is tough, but it saves trouble in the long run. On the other hand, everybody's got a right to keep their personal business private, and I respect that."

She visibly relaxed. "That's true."

He lifted an eyebrow. "Still not finished. I respect that except when it comes to my own people—the people I care about the most. Ruby heads up that list. And the rest of 'em follow right behind. Maggie, Torey, Ryder, Nick and Jina." He called the roll of his foster siblings quietly. "And you."

Her face crumpled. "Oh."

"You're one of my oldest friends, and one of the best, and I promised your doctor I was going to take good care of you. So I need to know why me going on a routine domestic call is giving you panic attacks."

She looked at him, still nibbling on her bottom lip the way she'd always done when she was uncertain. He watched her think it over. "I don't want to talk about it," she whispered finally.

He leaned back in the recliner. "I can see that. But we've always been able to talk to each other about anything. Haven't we?"

"Yes." She studied her hands, clenched together over the mound of her stomach. She was silent for a few ticks of the old clock on the wall. Then she took in a deep breath and looked back up at him.

"My marriage got really…difficult toward the end. Dylan had problems, especially when it came to alcohol. When he'd been drinking…" She paused and he saw her knuckles go white as she clamped down. "Sometimes things got physical."

Logan's heart fell. He'd known—or he'd been about 90 percent sure. Still, hearing Charlotte say the words out loud slammed him harder than he'd expected.

"He hit you?" He was able to keep his voice level, another perk of his professional training. Sometimes when you wanted people to keep talking, you couldn't let on how you were feeling.

He definitely wanted Charlotte to keep talking.

"A few times." She caught his eye and amended, "More than a few times."

He felt sick. If he'd known—if he'd so much as suspected. But he hadn't.

"Did you ever call the law on him?"

"A couple of times."

"And?"

"It just made things worse. Once Dylan started waving a gun around. He'd never done that before, but he was so mad at me for calling 911." Charlotte swallowed hard. "They arrested him, but all charges were dropped later."

Logan frowned. "That's impossible. No officer would drop those charges."

Charlotte laughed humorlessly. "Nothing's impossible in Savannah when your last name is Tremaine."

He remembered the self-important, perfectly dressed woman who'd come into Charlotte's barren hospital room and tightened his jaw. "I wish you'd called me. I know I told you not to." That memory felt like a kick in the gut now. "So, it's my own fault you didn't. But I sure wish you had."

He was talking to himself more than Charlotte, but she answered him anyway.

"Don't blame yourself, Logan. You couldn't have helped me. My situation was too complicated."

He'd been gazing off at the fireplace, thinking about Dylan. He snapped his head back around and looked at her. She seemed embarrassed.

"I'd have helped you. I'd have found a way."

"You're mad."

Yeah, he was, and the shamed look on her face was only making him madder.

"Not at you. I've seen too many people caught in situations like yours not to understand how tricky they can be. But, believe me, if I'd had any idea what was going on, I'd have done everything I could to get you out of there." He *would* have gotten her out of there. If he'd had to knock down Dylan, his mother and every last member of Savannah's high society to keep Charlotte safe, he wouldn't have hesitated. He paused. "Dylan's mother. I'm guessing she wasn't supportive. What'd she do? Cover everything up?"

"Yes. It took all the clout she had to keep things quiet, but she managed it."

"And blamed you."

She didn't answer, but she didn't have to. He knew he was right.

"You don't have to go back there. Ever. You know that, don't you?"

"I don't want to."

"Then you won't. I'll help you go anywhere you want to, do anything you want. I don't have as much money as the Tremaines, but I have some. We'll figure it out."

"Oh, but I can't—"

"Sure, you can. Right now, though, you're pregnant, and that constitutes special circumstances. So for the time being, you're going to let me and Ruby look after you. If you want me to talk to Mrs. Tremaine, I'll do it." Gladly.

"No, I'll talk to her myself when I'm ready. I've known for some time that I needed to put distance between us, move out of her house...maybe even leave Savannah altogether. I knew how she'd react, though, and I've been dreading telling her. I've been ignoring her calls ever since I've been here."

"Good for you. You needed a little time to relax. Speaking of that, don't lose any more sleep over me. Thanks to my dad and his shady friends, I learned how to disarm a drunk before I was thirteen, and I've had years of professional training since then. I can look after myself." He stood and held out a hand. "Come on. I'll drive you back to Ruby's."

She took his hand and leveraged herself off the sofa. "Thanks. I'm sorry to put you to so much trouble."

"It's no trouble." A loop of her hair worked loose from her ponytail to curl beside her cheek. Before he thought better of it, he reached out and tucked it behind her ear.

She flinched reflexively, and Logan gritted his teeth. If Dylan Tremaine wasn't already in his grave...

But he was, and Charlotte was safe now. Sooner or later, she'd understand that.

"We'd better hurry," he said. "If I don't get you back before dawn, Ruby'll be calling the preacher and setting up a shotgun wedding for sure."

He was only trying to lighten the mood, but when he saw the shift in Charlotte's expression, he knew his joke hadn't been a good idea.

"I'll never get married again, Logan."

"I was just kidding."

"I'm not." She spoke flatly. "And I don't think Ruby is, either. Since you mentioned her matchmaking ideas, I've noticed a few things. She's definitely trying to start something between us."

He opened the cabin door and ushered her out into the crisp night air. "She can try," he said amiably. "Won't do any good. Marriage isn't in my plans." He settled her into the front of his truck and doubled back to the driver's side.

"Ever?" Charlotte asked as he stuck the key into the ignition.

"Huh?" He flipped on the headlights and looked over his shoulder as he backed up.

"I mean, obviously I have my reasons. Plus," she rubbed her baby bump, "I'm not on my own anymore. I have my son to think about, and I couldn't risk marrying somebody who might not treat him well."

"I can understand that." Logan put the truck into gear and started down the dark dirt road. He had a suspicion that Dylan would've been worse than the average stepfather, but he left that thought unspoken.

"You've never been married, though. Why aren't you interested in finding somebody, maybe starting a family of your own?"

He shot her a sideways look. "That's an essay question, Charlotte, and it's late."

"Give me the bullet points."

He sighed. "I guess I've seen marriage go south too many times. I mean, take the couple I had to deal with tonight. I guarantee you they'll be back together again by this time tomorrow. I can also guarantee you that I'll be called back to their residence before the month's out to break up another brawl." He stopped at the fork and turned the truck toward the farm. "My own father changed wives like other men change socks. He'd charm a woman so much that she'd forget her good sense, marry him, then find out what a bad bargain she'd made once it was too late. He'd empty her bank account, she'd divorce him and then the whole process would start all over again."

"You've never told me much about your father."

"There's a reason for that." He pulled up beside the farmhouse. "Maybe a century or two ago, when people were more practical about marriage, I could have gotten on board, but all this romance stuff seems pretty flimsy to me."

"You mean when you could have traded a sack of potatoes and a cow and gotten yourself a bride? You really think that would have ended up better?"

He looked at her. In the moonlight coming through the window, he could see she was smiling at him. Teasing him.

That was good. He smiled back.

"I'd have traded two cows. I'd have wanted a really good one."

She sputtered a laugh. "At least you have standards."

He grinned. "Wait there. I'll walk you up to the porch."

She had the door open before he made it around. "I can manage," she said, trying to push herself out of the truck.

"Careful." He reached out to steady her.

Once again, she recoiled at the sudden movement. He understood why, but it didn't make him hate it any less. He set his jaw and cupped his hand gently under her elbow, helping her down from the high seat of the truck.

Neither of them spoke as he escorted her to the steps. He walked with her, only releasing her arm when she was safely on the porch.

"Thanks." She kept her eyes averted.

"I'm not like Dylan, Charlotte. I'd never hurt you."

He hadn't meant to say that. He'd only meant to say good-night, but somehow those words had come out instead.

She lifted her chin and looked at him, her face edged

silver in the moonlight. Her mouth twisted, and she suddenly looked a lot older.

"No, you wouldn't," she agreed quietly. "Not on purpose. I know that. Good night, Logan."

As he waited for her to go into the house, he caught a flutter of movement in his peripheral vision. Ruby was peeking through her bedroom window, spotlighted in the headlights.

She gave a little wave, then stepped back, letting the curtain fall into place.

He shook his head as he climbed into the truck. Ruby's matchmaking antics were frustrating, but at least now he knew he and Charlotte were on the same page. His foster mom had picked two nonstarters this time. Nothing was going to happen between them, no matter how many stunts Ruby pulled.

He nosed the truck back down the sloping driveway. Knowing Charlotte had no more interest in romance than he did made things simpler. He should be feeling relieved. Happy even.

Instead, he just felt tired.

It had been a really tough night.

Three days later, Charlotte sat with Ruby on the front porch of the farmhouse, piecing quilt squares and feeling more at peace with the world than she had in years.

The phone she'd charged and tucked in her pocket at Logan's insistence chirred irritably. She pulled it out and sneaked a look.

Elizabeth again. Charlotte put the phone away. She wasn't going to let her mother-in-law ruin this pretty afternoon.

It was a beautiful day. Well past noon, but not too hot. The mountain breezes stirred the air, bringing the coolness of hidden springs drifting against her cheek. She'd been hot and miserable in Savannah, but she felt so much better here. Calmer, too, especially since her talk with Logan the other night.

She'd been dreading telling him how bad things had been in her marriage, but she shouldn't have worried. Logan wasn't the kind of man to say "I told you so." There was something reassuring about him. A person looked at those broad shoulders and those clear, steady eyes and knew that this man could be trusted.

Being with Logan felt comfortable, like pulling her hair into a ponytail and padding around in sock feet. After three years of feeling jumpy and uneasy, this was a welcome change.

The phone chirred again.

"You ever planning to answer that thing?" Ruby asked.

"Eventually."

Ruby chuckled. "No love lost there, I see. You're only making it worse, you know, dodging her calls. You need to face up to her."

"I know. I've texted her." Three times, in response to repeated calls and a spate of increasingly snippy messages. Elizabeth wasn't used to people ignoring her. "I need a little space right now. Oh!" An idea occurred to her, and she threw a worried glance in Ruby's direction. "I hope I'm not overstaying my welcome."

"Don't you worry about that. You're welcome to stay here just as long as you've a mind to. Although," Ruby added, "if you're planning on staying much longer, we need to set up that appointment with Dr. Woods, the doctor who delivered Gracie. Logan says that's what your Savannah doctor expected you to do, and we want to be real careful."

"All right." She'd been thinking about that. The idea of starting over with a new obstetrician at this late stage wasn't appealing. On the other hand, neither was going back to Savannah. "If you'll give me his number, I'll make the appointment."

"Good." Ruby nodded. "If you're nervous, Maggie would go with you to your first appointment, I'm sure. Or Logan could, if you'd rather have him. That boy's got a knack for making folks feel safe, ain't he?"

Funny how she'd just been thinking that same thing. Sometimes Ruby was a little too perceptive.

Charlotte kept her eyes fixed on her quilt square, putting in the final stitch and clipping the thread. Time to change the subject. "These squares are turning out really well." She smoothed the finished piece over the mound of her belly. "Once you finish the one you're working on, we'll only have the corner ones to do. Then it'll be time to piece the top together. Are you going to want to use the machine for that? It'd be quicker."

"I don't think so. Makes it more personal, setting the stitches in by hand. It's going to mean the world to Logan, knowing you and me did this ourselves. Don't you think?"

Charlotte sidestepped the question. "It's going to be beautiful." She traced the triangular points of her square with one finger, remembering the shirt this bit had come from. It had started out legal-pad yellow, but Logan had worn it until it had faded into the palest of golds. Good thing, because now the color melded perfectly with the other fabrics. It was soft, too, washed so many times that the material had felt like a whisper when she'd held it against her cheek.

"You know, you could stay in Cedar Ridge. For good, I mean."

Charlotte glanced up. Ruby had her glasses perched on the end of her nose, and she'd tilted her head back so that she could peer at Charlotte through them.

"Oh," Charlotte protested weakly. "I don't know…"

"Why not? It's a good town to raise children in. I should know. I raised six of 'em. And it would put some breathing room between you and that mother-in-law of yours. Some relationships do better that way."

"That's true." Elizabeth's bossiness was easier to cope with at a distance, that much was for sure. But staying away from Savannah was going to cost money, and that was a problem. Dylan had gambled away her inheritance from her grandparents and left their finances in an awful mess.

"You're worrying about money. Don't bother to deny it, honey. I know that look. Had it on my own face more than once. That's no problem. Why don't you stay until after the baby's born? Once he's arrived safe and sound, and you're feeling like yourself again, we'll find you a job. There's plenty of brides needing dresses around here. Maybe you can start up your sewing business again."

Charlotte remembered Pippa and shuddered. "To tell you the truth, I've just about had enough of weddings."

Ruby lifted a skimpy eyebrow. "Is that so? Pity. Well, there's other things. People are always needing clothes altered, and I know plenty who'd pay a pretty penny for a quilt like this one here. And I've noticed the costumes at the church plays at Christmastime and Easter are looking mighty seedy. I'm sure you'd find lots to do. And who knows? Weddings may start to appeal to you again before too much longer, 'specially if you meet the right fellow."

The phone vibrated again. Elizabeth was persistent, and Ruby was right. She'd have to deal with her mother-in-law soon.

But there was something else she needed to deal with first.

"Ruby, I understand how much you want to see Logan

settled. He's explained that to me—how you like to match-make for your kids. But you're barking up the wrong tree. I love Logan to death—as a friend. I always will. But I'm not interested in getting married again." She started to add that Logan wasn't interested in marriage either but stopped herself. That might be the truth, but it wasn't her place to tell it.

"I wouldn't pay too much attention to that feeling. You're too young to give up on marriage altogether."

The phone made a blurping sound, warning Charlotte that Elizabeth had left another voice mail criticizing her choice to leave Savannah. Suddenly, it all seemed just a little too much.

"I know exactly how I feel, Ruby," Charlotte said firmly. "About Logan and about marriage."

"Sure you do. I'm not disputing that. And you got good reasons for those feelings. But feelings change."

"Ruby—"

"You just got to trust all those old hurts and disappointments and fears to God, honey. That's the answer."

"I do trust God—or I'm trying to. But He's not going to erase the past."

"'Course not." Ruby chuckled. "That'd be a waste. God never wastes our hurts, but He sure ain't shy about using them as a starting place. If you give Him the chance, He'll take all that ugliness and turn it into something real special. Like this." Ruby placed her completed square along-side Charlotte's on the table between their rockers and tapped it with one gnarled finger. "Until you came along, wasn't nothing here but some worn-out old shirts. But be-tween you and me, we're turning those scraps into some-thing beautiful, aren't we? That's nothing compared to what the Lord can do. You'll see. In God's good time, you'll see." She winked. "I'm praying you'll also see that a good friend can turn into a fine husband."

"Ruby!" Charlotte shot her friend an exasperated look.

"All right, all right." Ruby pushed herself up from the rocking chair. "I'll hush. One thing I've learned, it ain't a good idea to yank the steering wheel out of the good Lord's hands. Gotta give Him plenty of time to work. I'm going to go inside and get us some lemonade and cookies. We've done a lot of good sewing, and it's past time for a snack."

"I'll help." Charlotte made a move to get up.

"You'll do no such thing. You stay right there and let yourself be waited on. I won't be a minute."

As Ruby disappeared into the house, Charlotte's phone buzzed again.

"Might as well answer that and get it over with," Ruby called.

Charlotte sighed, but Ruby was right. Now was as good a time as any. She'd deal with Elizabeth and reward herself afterward with lemonade and cookies. She pulled out the phone and frowned at the contact information showing on her screen.

That wasn't Elizabeth's number. The caller was the Tremaine's lawyer, Lou Findley. The last time she'd heard from Lou, it had been to settle out Dylan's estate—which had mostly amounted to setting up payments for his debts.

"Hello?" she said.

Ten minutes later, Ruby walked back out on the porch.

"I've fixed us up a tray. Logan told Maggie to bake oatmeal raisin cookies 'cause he thinks they sound healthier. The good news is, my girl makes 'em taste as good as the chocolate chip ones. Ain't everybody can pull that off, but she can. Charlotte? You all right?"

Charlotte heard her talking, but the words seemed to be coming from far away.

"Honey?" There was a rattling as Ruby stooped to set the laden tray on the small table. The old woman taking Charlotte's hand in her cool ones. "What's wrong? Is it the baby?"

Charlotte looked into Ruby's concerned face and shook her head. She knew Ruby wanted more of an explanation, but she couldn't speak. She was having too much trouble breathing—the more she gasped, the less air she seemed able to suck in.

"Breathe slow, honey. Deep and slow." Ruby held out her hand. "Everything's going to be just fine. Give me that phone."

Mutely, Charlotte handed it over. The lawyer had hung up already anyway.

Ruby squinted at the device, punched a few numbers, then held it to her ear.

"Hey, there, Marla. Ruby Sawyer. My boy there in the office or out on patrol? Well, get him on that radio of yours and tell him he needs to come home. Yes, now. No, don't send an ambulance. Just Logan's all we need." Ruby stroked Charlotte's cheek. "And Marla? Tell him I said to hurry."

Chapter Seven

Logan got Ruby's message just as he was finishing up a call from an eighty-five-year-old widow, convinced a vagrant had holed up in her backyard shed. The intruder turned out to be a stray cat who'd increased the feline population by seven, all in varying shades of orange.

Edna McDonald was delighted with her new pets, so all was well. At least until Marla relayed that Ruby had requested his presence back at the house.

"10-18," the dispatcher added, making Logan's heart-rate ramp up.

In radio speak 10-18 meant get there fast, and he didn't wait to be told twice. He called goodbye to Edna, jumped into the patrol car and spun down her gravel drive.

"Roane County, 10-52 at that location," he ordered. *Send the ambulance.* He didn't know whether it was Charlotte or Ruby herself in trouble, but either way, he wanted medical personnel on-site, pronto.

"Caller says that's not necessary."

Logan gritted his teeth and pressed harder on the gas pedal. "I repeat—10-52."

"10-4." All his officers knew better than to express personal opinions on the radio, but he heard the warning in Marla's voice as plainly as if she'd spelled it out.

Ruby's going to be mad.

He hoped so. He truly hoped so, because that meant the ambulance really wasn't necessary. That's what he was praying for.

He blew past the speed limit posted on the road leading up Sawyer's mountain, and he pulled into the drive six minutes after he'd received Marla's call.

Ruby and Charlotte were on the porch. Ruby hovered over Charlotte, fanning her with one of her big palmetto "church fans."

So, it was Charlotte, then. Logan's stomach did a nauseating flip and dip. Thankfully, he could hear the wail of the ambulance in the distance. They'd get here quick. They always did.

He jogged toward the porch, clearing the steps in one stride.

"What's going on?" he asked. Charlotte was pale as a sheet and breathing raggedly. "Is it the baby?"

"She says not," Ruby answered. Charlotte seemed very focused on getting her breath. "She's having one of those panic attacks, poor thing, like she did that night you got called out to the Wilsons'. Oh, don't look at me like that. There aren't any secrets in a small town. Anyhow, Charlotte hasn't been able to tell me too much yet, but it's something connected to her mother-in-law, I believe."

His foster mother raised her head, listening. "Logan! You didn't drag those poor ambulance folks all the way out here? I told Marla we didn't need them."

"I outrank you, Ruby, at the sheriff's office, anyway. You call and tell me to get here fast without any explanation, you're getting the ambulance, too." He crouched in front of Charlotte. "Hey," he said gently. "What happened? Can you tell me?"

Her eyes slid to his, and as they connected, her face crumpled. "She wants to take my baby."

"What?"

"The lawyer called. He says she's starting the paper-work now. She's saying I have no means of support. That I'm…unstable and unfit. She wants me to sign papers giv-ing her custody as soon as he's born."

Logan felt a surge of angry disgust. Apparently Dylan's rotten apple hadn't fallen far from the maternal tree. "She's bluffing, Charlotte, trying to scare you back to Savannah. She can't really take your baby."

She shook her head. "You don't know Elizabeth. She al-ways gets what she wants. She's already cut off my health insurance, the lawyer says. She was helping with that—I couldn't afford a good policy, and she wanted the best doc-tors for Dylan's baby. I don't… I don't know what to do."

"You're going to fight back." Logan spoke with a grim certainty. "And so am I." He picked up Charlotte's cell phone and looked for recent calls. "This Findlay, he's the lawyer?"

She nodded as the shrill sirens grew louder, echoing off the side of the mountain.

"The best person to square off with a lawyer is another lawyer. And I know just the guy. Eric Dawson. I'm going to give him a call right now."

"But lawyers cost so much, and I don't have—"

"Don't worry about that. This guy's a good friend of mine, and he owes me a favor. We'll ask his opinion to start with, and go from there." He dug his own phone out of his pocket as the ambulance pulled up in the yard. Two male paramedics bailed out of the cab and raced toward the house.

Logan threw up a hand, and the medics slowed, looking at him questioningly.

"Nice and easy, guys. She's eight months pregnant, and she's had a shock. She's had some blood pressure problems in the past, so take a close look at that." He patted Charlotte's arm. "Dean and Marcus here will check you over, make sure everything's all right."

Charlotte threw the men an apprehensive look. "Oh, Logan, I just found out I don't have medical insurance, and I don't think—"

"I'll cover the cost. I'm the one who overruled Ruby and called them. Now, these fellows are good guys, and they've driven all the way up here. Just let them do their jobs." When she still hesitated, he added, "Humor me."

"Might as well, honey," Ruby muttered. "This one's too stubborn for his own good—and bossy as a bantam rooster." That last part was delivered with a narrow glance at him. He ignored it.

"While they take care of you, I'll call Eric. We'll start getting this mess straightened out."

He waited until she nodded. Then he stood and backed away, allowing the paramedics to approach.

"Stay with her," he instructed Ruby. "I'll be right back."

He walked until he was out of earshot and made his call. Eric's secretary put him straight through, and he gave the local attorney the phone number he'd found on Charlotte's phone along with the small amount of information he had.

"Call you back," Eric said brusquely and hung up.

Less than ten minutes later, Logan's phone buzzed.

As usual Eric didn't pull any punches. "Your friend's got trouble," he announced. "Lou Findlay's a power player, and all his clients have political influence and money to burn. This guy's a force to be reckoned with, Logan."

"Maybe so, but come on, Eric. No matter how good her lawyer is, this woman can't take Charlotte's baby, surely."

"It won't be easy, but I wouldn't rule it out. Findlay has a reputation of playing fast and loose with ethics, but he wins his cases and that's all that matters to the people who hire him. He took my call himself, and that lets me know he's taking this client seriously. And he wouldn't have accepted the case at all, probably, if he didn't feel confident he can bulldoze another win out of it."

This wasn't sounding good. "What should she do?"

"I don't know. It looks pretty grim. He mentioned a nervous breakdown at some society wedding, no health insurance—"

"Because his client canceled it. And her son was an abusive husband, Eric. That ought to count for something."

"Do you have proof?"

Logan remembered what Charlotte had said about the power of the Tremaine name. "Probably not."

"Then I can't use it. That's too bad because they're collecting their ammo, and she's going to need to return fire. If this case matters to you, I'll be happy to help her out, pro bono."

"I can't let you do that."

"Can't stop me, either." He could hear Eric's grin over the phone. "You've helped me a time or two, so I'm glad to return the favor. Plus, to tell you the truth, I wouldn't mind going up against Findlay. It'll give me a chance to stretch my muscles. But I won't mislead you, he's got the power and the experience to outgun me."

"The truth's on your side."

"It is. But you and I both know sometimes that doesn't matter as much as it should."

Good point. Logan watched the scene on the front porch, pondering what Eric had said. The paramedics appeared to be done with Charlotte now, and since they weren't loading her on a stretcher, things must not be too bad.

That was something anyway. But once she heard this news, he had a feeling things would go south in a hurry.

"Logan?" Eric interrupted his thoughts. "Pardon me for getting personal, but are you and this woman romantically involved?"

His attention abruptly refocused on the phone. "There's nothing like that going on. If they're insinuating—"

"Nobody's insinuating anything. I was going in the opposite direction. It would actually work for her if you two were a couple."

"What do you mean?"

"According to what Findlay said, they're banking on her low income level, her lack of health insurance and her inability to provide a stable environment for this baby. But hey, you're about as stable as they come. Government job, steady paycheck, good insurance. Plus—" Eric hesitated.

"What?"

"Well, if you and she were serious about each other, it could throw the whole custody squabble into a new light. No matter how much influence this woman has, it's going to look like she's just mad because her late son's kid is getting a new daddy. And if that daddy's a Georgia sheriff with your track record? She wouldn't have a leg to stand on, and any judge would think twice before awarding her custody. If you two were a committed couple, I could win this case without breaking a sweat, Findlay or no Findlay."

He had Logan's full attention now. "Committed couple. You mean, like engaged?"

"Maybe. Married would be a sure thing, but engaged might work. Anyhow, just thinking out loud. Since that's not the situation, we'll have to go with what we have. I won't lie, Logan. It'll be an uphill slog with a guy like

Findlay at the helm. She might as well know what she's up against."

Logan studied Charlotte, sitting in the rocking chair. As he watched, she rubbed her eyes wearily with one hand. "Let me get this straight. As things stand, Charlotte faces a real danger of losing custody of her own baby to Dylan's mother, even though she hasn't done anything wrong."

"Yeah. Sorry, but that's the truth as I see it."

"But if she and I were married, Mrs. Tremaine and her fancy lawyer wouldn't be able to pull it off."

"Right. I could pretty much guarantee a custody case would swing Charlotte's way then, but since you two aren't—" There was a pause on the other end of the phone. "Wait just a minute. Logan, you're not thinking—"

"We'll talk again tomorrow, Eric." Logan ended the call and walked toward the porch, his mind whirling.

He wasn't sure—yet—what he was going to do, or what Charlotte would say, or how this would all play out. Right now, he was only sure of one thing.

Nobody was taking Charlotte's baby away from her, not if he could help it.

"I don't understand." The following morning, Charlotte frowned at Logan as she struggled to adjust the truck's seat belt over her baby bump. "Why do you keep pestering me about whether or not I have my Social Security card? I thought we were just going out for breakfast."

She wished she hadn't let him talk her into this. She knew he was only trying to cheer her up, but she really didn't feel up to it. Even though Ruby had insisted on dosing her with a big mug of herbal tea, she'd spent the night tossing and turning, worrying over what Findlay had told her. In the fitful snatches of sleep she'd managed, she'd dreamed terrible dreams.

The fact that Logan had been so cagey about what his lawyer friend thought about her chances hadn't helped. She didn't want to go anywhere right now, and she sure didn't feel like eating. All she wanted to do was find someplace to hide, hopefully somewhere Elizabeth couldn't find her.

"We *are* going for breakfast. First." He glanced at her, then turned his attention back to the road. "Then I've got something else planned."

"What's that?"

"I'll explain everything while we eat. Do you have the card with you or not?"

She sighed and shifted the seat belt again, trying to find a comfortable position. It was a waste of time. There wasn't one. The bigger she got, the more of a problem everything became. "You said to bring it and my driver's license, so yes, I do. But I don't understand why I need it."

"I'd rather not get into it while we're driving. The restaurant's not far, just over the Tennessee line." He shot her another quick look. "Mama Berry's. Remember? That was always one of your favorite places."

"Oh, Mama B's!" In spite of her worries and her discomfort, Charlotte's mouth tipped up into her first real smile since that awful phone call. "I love her blueberry pancakes."

He smiled back. "I know."

Charlotte felt a twinge of guilt. He was trying so hard to make her happy. He'd even taken the whole day off work, which Ruby assured her he never did, so he could treat her to this breakfast—and whatever else he'd planned. No telling what that was. He'd been acting weird ever since Ruby had called him out to the house yesterday.

Charlotte winced as the baby moved and kicked—she wasn't the only one getting uncomfortable these days. Well, whatever Logan was up to, she'd find out soon enough.

And actually, blueberry pancakes didn't sound half bad.

Mama Berry's was only a thirty-minute drive from Cedar Ridge, so they were soon pulling into the parking lot. The tiny eatery was pleasantly busy but not too crowded, and all decorated for autumn. Corn stalks were lashed together and spaced along the porch, along with hay bales and bright orange pumpkins. A chubby scarecrow wearing a bonnet and a calico dress perched on one of the bales, holding a sign that read, Welcome to Mama Berry's! Mind Your Manners and Eat Your Fill!

The fall colors clashed with Mama B's unusual choice of magenta paint for her siding, but what did that matter? The restaurant looked exactly as she remembered it, and Charlotte felt her spirits lifting even before Logan had switched off the engine.

She smiled as he came around to open the passenger door. "This place looks exactly the same. Do you think Mama's still here?"

"Are you kidding?" He carefully helped her down. "Mama won't leave that griddle until they carry her out the door feet first. Come on."

He offered her his arm, and Charlotte took it. As they crossed the parking lot, she inhaled a breath of fresh mountain air—scented heavily with frying bacon. Her worries were immediately shoved aside, replaced with memories of the countless fun Saturday mornings she'd spent here with Logan. She squeezed his hand and laid her head briefly against his arm. "I'm sorry I was so grumpy earlier. This was a really sweet thing for you to do."

"Were you grumpy?" He cut her an amused glance. "I didn't notice."

Charlotte snorted and swatted him.

Once inside, they called an enthusiastic hello to Mama Janice Berry, who was manning the wide griddle and popping her chewing gum in time to the gospel music on the radio. When the heavy-set woman caught sight of them, she hollered so loudly that all the customers in the small room jumped and stared.

"Look what the cat dragged in! Oh, I got to hug your necks. Phyllis, watch these pancakes for a minute. Mind now, I just turned 'em." The sixtysomething restaurant owner squeezed around the counter and enveloped Charlotte in a soft, blueberry scented embrace.

"Girl, girl, girl," the older woman murmured in her ear. "It's so good to see you! You've stayed away too long."

"It's good to see you too, Mama B," Charlotte whispered past the lump in her throat. Small towns had their advantages. She'd forgotten what it felt like to be hugged and welcomed like a movie star everywhere you went. When Mama finally released her, Charlotte laughed self-consciously and scrubbed at her teary eyes. "You haven't changed a bit."

"Can't say the same about you." Mama Berry stepped back and looked down at Charlotte's rounded middle with a grin. "You're just about to pop, aren't you? My, my! You were always such a little bitty thing, even though you ate my pancakes like a truck driver. And look at you now! All right, you two, go on and find yourself a table. No, no, you don't need a menu—I know what you want better'n you do. Phyllis! Pour some more batter out on that griddle! We got two more tall stacks to make."

Logan led the way to a table crammed into the farthest corner, shielded from the rest of the room by a half wall decorated with pictures of pigs. He pulled out a chair, and Charlotte considered it dubiously.

"Won't we be kind of cramped over here?" She ran a hand down her middle with a rueful smile. "I'm not sure I can fit behind that table. Maybe we should try a booth."

"We need privacy." Logan pulled the table out an extra foot from the wall. "There. Plenty of room for both of you now."

"All right." Charlotte shrugged and sat in the offered chair. "Privacy, huh?" She pulled a few napkins out of the dispenser and handed him a couple. They both liked lots of syrup on their pancakes, and things got pretty drippy at Mama B's. "I guess that explains why you brought me here instead of going to Angelo's and letting Maggie make our pancakes." She lowered her voice and leaned in close. "Don't tell Mama B, but I'm sure Maggie could make pancakes almost as good as the ones here." She straightened up and smiled. "I don't think you'd get much privacy with your sister around, though."

"Not likely. Maggie would probably plop herself right down at the table with us." Logan fidgeted with his napkin, folding and unfolding it. "She wouldn't be the only one, either. Whenever I sit down to eat in Cedar Ridge, I end up cornered by somebody who wants to complain about a parking ticket or a loud neighbor."

"I didn't think about that." She'd been so caught up in her own problems that she'd forgotten what a load of responsibility Logan carried. "I don't blame you for wanting to have a peaceful breakfast out of town."

He shot her a rueful look. "It may not be so peaceful once I explain—"

"Here's your coffee." Mama B swooped over with a carafe in each hand.

"Oh, thanks, but I shouldn't—" Charlotte started.

"Relax, honey. This ain't my first rodeo. Decaf for you. Pancakes'll be up in a jiffy, and I'm putting a little bit of bacon on your plate for a treat. Not much, and it's that all-natural kind. Phyllis is frying it up special now. You'll get the regular stuff," Mama B informed Logan with wink.

"Good."

"You sure found yourself a cozy corner over here." The older woman winked. "I always did think you two made a cute couple. I know, I know." She rolled her eyes. "You're just friends. I've heard it all before, and going by that baby bump, it looks like Logan here missed his chance, but I'm still entitled to my opinion. Back in a minute." She hurried off again.

Charlotte stirred a splash of creamer into her coffee, studying Logan. He was fiddling with his napkin again. "All right. We've got our privacy, and the pancakes are on their way. Tell me about this secret plan of yours."

"Maybe we should eat first."

She frowned. "You're stalling." She'd lifted her coffee cup to take a sip, but now she set it back on its fat little saucer with a clink. "That's not like you. You're starting to make me nervous. What's going on?"

He leaned back in his chair and studied her. "I don't know exactly how to tell you this," he muttered.

"How to tell me what?" She tilted her head, looking at him. "Spit it out, Logan. What exactly do you want us to do today?"

He set his jaw and met her eyes. "I think we should get married."

Crash! Charlotte turned to find Mama B staring at the two laden plates she had dropped on the floor. The older woman looked up, and for once she seemed speechless.

Charlotte understood that feeling. This was a speechless moment, for sure.

"I'll have Fred clean this up," Mama muttered finally, her cheeks blooming a mottled red. "And I'll…uh…bring you some more pancakes. Phyllis!" she bellowed as she hurried back toward the stove.

Charlotte shifted around in her chair and faced Logan. "You. Start explaining."

Chapter Eight

"Eric gave me the idea," Logan started. He paused as Fred, the elderly busboy, came to clean up the mess of smashed dishes and pancakes.

"Go on," Charlotte prompted. The small restaurant had gone silent and the other customers were sneaking curious glances in their direction.

He pushed his chair back and stood. "I think our privacy is shot. Let's go outside. Mama B? Put those pancakes on hold for just a minute, will you?"

Mama B turned, her spatula in one hand. "No problem." She still looked shell-shocked.

Charlotte understood the feeling. As she followed Logan outside, she kept turning what he'd said over and over in her mind.

I think we should get married.

If he'd announced, "I think we should fly to Mars," she couldn't have been any more confused.

Outside Mama B's the air was still cool and bacon scented, but the comforting sense of familiarity was gone. Logan Carter had just proposed marriage out of the blue, and her whole world had slipped sideways.

He led the way to a cement picnic table underneath an

oak whose green leaves were just starting to tint yellow. He brushed some debris off the seat and motioned for her to sit. Charlotte sank onto the bench, its cold dampness seeping through her maternity jeans.

He sat across from her, propping his elbows on the rough slab of a table.

"First off, I'm sorry about dropping that bomb on you back there. I've been worrying over how to bring this up, but I never came up with a good way to explain it." He rubbed his chin and made a rueful face. "Obviously."

"You said you came up with this…bomb…because of something your lawyer friend told you?"

"Yes."

"Maybe you'd better start there."

He nodded, looking relieved at the suggestion. "Okay, so the bad news is that Eric thinks Mrs. Tremaine has a real shot at this custody angle she and her lawyer are working."

Charlotte's stomach fell, and panic crowded in. "I knew it!"

"Wait! There's good news, too. He's pretty sure we can stop them."

"How?" When Logan raised his eyebrows, Charlotte's panic shifted back to disbelief. "By getting married? You've got to be kidding."

"Nope, and to tell you the truth, it's actually a pretty smart idea."

Charlotte listened as he explained how their marriage could derail Elizabeth's plans in one move and make her look spiteful. Which, of course she was.

The truth of that registered in the logical part of her mind. The other half of her brain was still struggling to get a handle on all this.

"Marriage would make sense in other ways, too," he went on. "My insurance has excellent maternity benefits.

I looked it up. You'd be covered as soon as we were married. No waiting period. I checked on that, too. So you can go straight back home this afternoon and make that doctor's appointment you've been putting off."

"Today? You want us to get married *today*?"

"Right." He spoke as if this was the most reasonable idea in the world. "It shouldn't be a problem. Tennessee's a marriage-friendly state. I mean, we could've gotten married at the Cedar Ridge courthouse—there's no waiting period in Georgia anymore, either. But I know everybody there, and it would have turned into a circus. One of my deputies eloped to Tennessee last year, and he said it was the smartest decision he'd ever made. We can get married today, easily enough, with only the documentation we're carrying. No wait, no fuss, all done." He looked at his watch. "If we hurry, we could probably get the license before lunch."

"I'm sorry." Charlotte blinked and shook her head. "I'm…struggling to catch up here. This offer is really…" Okay. She had no idea what to call this. "I guess generous doesn't exactly cover it. And as—" Charlotte struggled to find the right word "—out there," she finished, "as this whole idea is, I suppose it's something we could talk over. Maybe. But, come on, Logan. We can't just get married. Today. Just like that." She snapped her fingers.

"Sure we can. I explained that. See, there's no waiting period—"

"No, no. I got that part." In spite of everything, she found herself fighting a desire to laugh. Sometimes Logan was such a—*guy*. "Legally, yes, I suppose we could."

"Okay." He waited, eyebrows lifted. "So, what's the problem?"

What's the problem? Was he serious? "Well, for starters, aren't you the guy who was telling me just the other day he had no intention of ever getting married?"

"Well, yeah." Logan blinked. "And I know you never planned to marry again, either. This is different. It wouldn't be that kind of a thing." He frowned at her. "You understand that, right? I'm not asking you to—I wouldn't expect…" He trailed off. "Our friendship is important to me. I'd never want anything to mess that up. We'd still be friends—who also happen to be married."

For the first time since this unbelievable conversation had started, Logan's idea actually sounded reasonable. Something stirred to life, way in the back in the furthest reaches of Charlotte's mind. Something almost…hopeful.

"Married friends," she repeated. That didn't sound so awful. "We get married but stay friends."

"Sure. Why not?"

She threw him a suspicious look. *Why not?* She had a checkered history with that question.

It was her favorite question to ask when she was working on a design project, debating on a not-so-traditional style or pattern or fabric. That one question had led her to create some of her very best work, work which was fresh and surprising and uniquely her own.

But that was art. The same question had also led her into some not-so-great life choices. Dylan came to mind.

Then again, Logan wasn't at all like Dylan.

She studied him—the straight, firm line of his jaw, so different from her late husband's softer one. The way his shoulders under the short-sleeved white shirt were set, so wide and strong. The way he edged ahead to open doors for her, his old-fashioned habit of pulling out her chairs. The way he insisted on walking her up steps and steadying her arm.

The way he'd driven all the way down to Savannah to

spend the night in an uncomfortable chair in her hospital room, because he'd remembered what it meant when she wore her mother's ring.

And the way he sat here now, offering her his life on a platter, because he couldn't bear the idea of standing by and doing nothing while she got hurt.

"Charlotte?"

She blinked. "I'm thinking."

"Is it starting to make more sense?"

"Maybe." She frowned. "I guess, if you strip away all the romantic stuff, a marriage boils down to a legal contract between two consenting adults." An idea occurred to her, and she glanced up at him, alarmed. "But Logan, there's something else."

"What's that?"

"I'm pregnant."

He lifted an eyebrow. "I've noticed."

"Have you thought about that?"

He sent her a quizzical look. "Charlotte, the baby's kind of the whole reason for this."

"No, I don't only mean keeping Elizabeth from getting custody." Although just saying those words out loud made a shiver of fear run up her spine. "I mean have you *really* thought about it. If we were married, you'd be my son's stepfather. If we go through with this, you won't just be taking me on, you'd be taking the baby on, too."

"I'm fine with that."

He still didn't understand. "Logan, you don't know Elizabeth like I do. This baby is her only grandchild, and with Dylan gone, she'll never have another one. She's not going to give up on this custody idea easily, and she has piles of money and plenty of clout. This could drag out for a long time. We might have to stay married for years."

"I realize that, and I'm prepared to see it through. However long it takes, Charlotte. We won't end the marriage until we're sure there's no more threat."

Still not getting it.

"But if my child spends years with you…if he learns to love you as his father, what's going to happen when…?"

Realization dawned in Logan's eyes. "If you're worried I'm going to duck out of your son's life as soon as our marriage is over, don't be. I'll be there for him as long as he wants me to be, whether you and I are married or not." When she didn't answer, he added, "I give you my word on that, Charlotte."

His word. She knew what that meant to him, how seriously Logan took it.

She also knew how seldom he gave it.

But still. "Logan, we're talking about a huge commitment."

"I understand that."

"That doesn't scare you?"

"Sure it does. I've never been anybody's dad before. I'm probably going to make some spectacular mistakes, and yeah, that scares me. What scares me more is the idea of another little boy growing up without a father in his life. I see too much of that in my line of work—enough to know that boys do better when they have a decent man who'll take up time with them. You say you never want to get married again. You never had a relationship with your dad, so he's not in the picture. You don't have any brothers who could step in. Dylan's father is dead I guess?"

She nodded. "Four years ago. Heart attack."

"Well, then. Who else has this kid got?"

She hadn't thought about that. To be honest, all she'd felt was a guilty relief that Dylan wasn't going to be in his son's life. She'd never considered the empty space that left open, or what that might mean for her little boy.

If that vacancy could be filled by a man like Logan… that would be a huge blessing. That alone was worth more than all the health insurance and legal stability in the whole wide world.

The hope that had been stirring in the back of her mind flexed its wings and stepped up into the light. This might actually work.

"I'm decent enough, but I'm not perfect," Logan was admitting with his usual honesty. "And like I said, I've never done this before. So, I get that this is a big leap of faith on your part. I hope I'll at least be better than nothing, but who knows what kind of dad I'll be?"

Oh.

She did.

Out of the blue, tears rushed hotly into her eyes because, yes. She knew.

She knew exactly what kind of father Logan would be, but it took her three tries to get the word out.

"Wonderful," she managed finally—and hiccupped a sob. He looked alarmed, but she waved a don't-worry-about-me hand at him. "You'll be a wonderful dad. Sorry. It's just…this is all a little much." She shook her head. "Don't mind me."

He rose and came around to her side of the picnic table. "Scootch over."

When she did, he sat down beside her and put one muscled arm around her shoulders, drawing her close to his chest. She felt him resting his chin on the top of her head, his hand gently rubbing up and down her upper arm.

And she smelled the faint, familiar scent of cedar.

"Everything's going to be okay, Charlotte." He spoke with such sureness that her whole body relaxed against him. Somehow, when this man said everything was going to be all right, you believed him.

"You're sure?" she asked, her words muffled against his chest. "You really want to do this?"

"I do."

His choice of words struck her as funny, and she spluttered a wet laugh into his shirt.

When she could speak again, she straightened up and looked him in the eye.

"Then you'd better go find a cow and some bags of potatoes because you just got yourself a bride."

He laughed and gave her shoulder a friendly squeeze.

"Two cows," he corrected with a wink. "Remember? 'Cause I'm getting a good one."

"That was fast," Charlotte said when they walked out of the county clerk's office. She looked bewildered.

"Like I told you, no wait, no fuss." As they stepped outside Logan opened the brochure he'd picked up. It unfolded to reveal the names of dozens of nearby wedding chapels. It was a confusing array of choices, so he quickly handed it off to her. "Pick one of these places, and we'll get everything finished up."

Charlotte stopped beside his truck and examined the list. "There sure are a lot of them."

"Weddings must be pretty profitable." He scanned the storefronts across the street from the brick courthouse. Various businesses filled the old-fashioned buildings, many of them with wedding related items in their windows. A florist, a clothing rental store, a pawn shop.

"They are," she murmured. "Trust me—I've worked my share of them over the past few years in all kinds of venues. Although," she added with a laugh, "none of them offered a drive-through option, best I recall. Three of these do." She handed him back the brochure. "You pick. It doesn't matter to me."

He accepted the list reluctantly. "Doesn't the bride usually pick the place?"

"The bride usually picks everything. Or her mother does." She gestured at her pink maternity smock and jeans. "But I'm not the usual bride. Look at me."

"There's nothing wrong with how you look." In fact, she looked adorable, standing there with her baby bump rounding out her shirt and her pale golden hair curving around her cheeks. He wasn't the only one who thought so. He'd noticed several people smiling at her, and more than one man shooting him an envious glance.

No surprise there. Charlotte looked like the girl-next-door-wife every guy dreamed about. Wholesome and sweet and fun.

She snorted and rolled her eyes. "Just pick a place, Logan."

He sighed, flipped the brochure over and glanced at the map. "The Sweetheart Chapel is closest. I can see if they have an opening today."

"Fine."

He punched in the number.

"Sure, honey." The woman who answered sounded pre-occupied, but pleasant. "We're pretty busy today, but we can fit you in around eleven-thirty, if that works for you."

Logan checked his watch. That gave them an hour to kill. "That'll be fine."

"You got any guests?"

"It's just the two of us."

"Okay, then. You'll need witnesses, but we can rustle somebody up for that. We got a flat-rate elopement fee. It's a hundred and twenty-five dollars. Cash or we take all major credit cards. Costs extra if you want photographs."

Logan shot an uncertain look at Charlotte. "I'm not sure what we'll want."

"No problem. Just let me know when you get here, and we'll set it up. We don't provide fresh flowers, but there's a silk bouquet your bride can borrow if she wants it. Bring your own rings, 'cause we don't sell those here. What are your names again?" She listened as Logan gave her the information. "Okay, I'm penciling you in, hon. Yeah, I'm coming, Mel. Just a minute! I got to hang up now. We got another couple ready to go. See you in a bit." The woman clicked off the line.

"We're on for eleven-thirty."

She lifted an eyebrow. "Just like that?"

"Just like that. We're supposed to let her know if we want photos when we get there."

She shook her head. "Well, this is eye-opening. Do you have any idea how long it usually takes to plan a wedding?"

"Not really." He tried to remember about Maggie and Neil's wedding, but his primary jobs in that scenario had been to carry heavy things around and show up on time.

"Well over a year, for the big ones. Hours and hours of coordinating with florists and caterers and stylists. You set everything up in less than an hour."

Did she mind about that? He couldn't tell. "It's pretty bare-bones, I know. I'm sorry, but I thought—"

"I wasn't complaining. I'm amazed at the efficiency of it. These quickie weddings are every bit as legal as the ones I worked on, with only a fraction of the trouble and cost." She shrugged. "Who knows? Maybe these work out better in the long run. Half the couples I've designed dresses for ended up in divorce courts, and the stress about their weddings probably didn't help. In fact, I noticed a connection—the more lavish the ceremony and reception, the quicker the marriage fell apart."

"Is that so?"

"My wedding to Dylan was considered the society event

of the season that year, if that tells you anything. And Elizabeth planned the whole thing." She smiled at him. "Okay, so we're on the books. What are we going to do for an hour?"

"We have a couple of errands to run. Come on." He helped her into the truck, and a minute later they were driving down the main street.

"This is the cutest town," Charlotte announced. "Nice architecture, but it's nothing fancy, and it's not trying to be. I like that." When he pulled into a parking slot, she looked at him. "Why are we stopping here?"

"We'll need rings."

"Oh." She considered the small jewelry store in front of them. "Are you sure you want to buy them here? I saw one of those toy machines in the courthouse lobby. We could probably score a ring there for a dollar."

He loved seeing that teasing look on her face again. He should have proposed marriage days ago. "Your finger would turn green in a week. You're the one who said this marriage might have to last awhile. We'd better get a ring that can last with it."

She looked down at her left hand. He realized with a start that she still wore her wedding set. She pulled off the flashy engagement ring and tucked it into her purse. "I have this one." She flicked her fingers so that the diamonds in the platinum band sparkled in the sunlight. "We could use it."

"No." He was surprised at how much he hated that idea. "We're not using your old one."

"It would make more sense than wasting money on a new one, wouldn't it?"

He didn't care how much sense it made. "I'd rather waste the money. And if you don't mind, maybe it would be a good idea to take that one off now." They were all wrong for Charlotte anyway, those gaudy rings. He didn't know what Dylan had been thinking.

"All right." She tugged it off and dropped it into her bag. "Maybe it won't cost much. We'll ask to see the cheapest ones."

Inside, the clerk produced a matching pair of simple gold wedding bands and stepped politely out of earshot. Logan looked at the rings with a faint sense of disappointment. He shouldn't have been so quick to judge Dylan. These weren't flashy, but they went too far in the other direction. They were too plain and ordinary—not like Charlotte at all.

It didn't matter, he reminded himself. The rings were just for show, anyhow.

Even so, if he'd had time, he'd have chosen ones that were different. Warm and unique and special.

When Logan asked her opinion, Charlotte frowned. "Those are cheaper." She pointed. "And they look almost the same."

"We'll take these," he called to the clerk, nodding at the pricier ones. "Ring them up together."

"I should pay for yours," she protested.

"Nope. Today's on me."

When they left the store, he glanced at his watch, then turned down the sidewalk instead of heading for the truck. Charlotte tugged at his arm.

"Where are we going now?"

"A bride should have flowers. I saw a florist about three doors up."

She stopped, looking surprised—and worried. "Oh, Logan. That's so thoughtful, but it's really not necessary."

"I think it is. The chapel lady said they have an artificial bouquet, but I know how you hate fake flowers."

"Still—it seems like another waste of money."

Her concern about finances nipped at his pride a little. "I can afford it. I'm not as rich as Dylan, maybe, but I've got a steady job and a healthy savings account." When she didn't budge, he tried a joke. "How do you think I afforded all those cows and potatoes?"

She didn't smile, so he added, "Relax. It's not going to be anything fancy. It can't be because they'll have to stick it all together in about twenty minutes."

"It's just… I don't want you to feel like you have to go to any extra trouble. It's not like I'm a real bride."

Something about the way she said that hit him in the center of his chest. "You're the only bride I'm ever likely to have, and I'd like to buy you some flowers. Okay?"

"Okay." She was nibbling on her lip again. "I guess. That's very sweet of you."

"Here." He walked her to a bench. "Why don't you sit down? You've been on your feet too much today. This shouldn't take long."

"Fine." She sat on the wooden seat with a tired *whuff*. "Are you going to be this bossy all the time once we're married? Maybe I should rethink this." She made a face at him.

She was joking. But it dawned on him that she was also right.

He'd been steamrolling her. With the best of intentions, true, but still.

Not okay.

He believed in tackling things like this head-on, so he dropped down on the bench beside her and answered her seriously.

"I'm sorry. You're right. I'm being bossy. And not just about the flowers and the rings, but about this whole plan. The truth is, what Eric said spooked me, and I wanted to get this all fixed up as quick as I could. But we don't have to do this today, Charlotte. The marriage license is good for a month. If you want to go back to the farm and think it over, we can do that. My offer will stand. It's completely up to you."

She stared at him from her spot on the bench, and her mouth worked. He couldn't quite decide if she was trying not to laugh—or not to cry.

"Go buy me some flowers," she whispered.

So, he did. And when he walked out fifteen minutes later with a small bouquet, she stood to accept it.

"I told them you were wearing pink." It looked pretty enough to him. There were roses. He recognized those. There were some green vines trailing out and some fluffy white flowers mixed in there, too. All in all, he didn't think it was too bad for a last-minute thing, but what did he know?

She looked over the blooms at him. "It's absolutely perfect, and I love it. Thank you very much."

But he saw a tiny glint of worry in her eyes. And she didn't say another word until they arrived at the wedding chapel.

"This is it," he said. He scanned the place through the windshield of the truck. It looked all right. It was built like a tiny log cabin, and there was a grapevine wreath shaped like a heart hanging on its front. A path of flat rocks led the way to the door, and it was sprinkled heavily with birdseed. "Last chance to reconsider. Are we doing this or not?"

"I want to." She looked at him, her brow furrowed. "I really do. But there's just one thing…"

"What?"

"What you said back there about me being your only bride…it made me think. This is a wonderful deal for me and my baby. But are you sure—I mean really sure—that *you* want to do this?"

"It was my idea."

"I know. But…" She looked at the bouquet of flowers in her lap and then back at him. "I've been married. I had the whole experience, the wedding, marrying a man I loved."

A man who hurt you, Logan thought, but he kept his mouth shut.

As usual, though, he didn't have to spell out his thoughts for Charlotte. "It didn't work out well," she admitted. "But, still. I had my romance. I know this marriage is temporary, and I understand why it makes sense. And I…well, it doesn't seem enough to tell you I appreciate it. What I feel goes a lot deeper than gratitude. But I also feel like I'm…cheating you out of something important. Something special."

"You aren't."

"I know you don't think you'll ever find somebody, but what if you do? If we do this, and then you find that right woman, you'll have this sham of a marriage behind you and a stepson, too. It might be kind of hard to explain."

"Stop." When she started to say more, he reached across the cab of the truck and put his finger against her lips. "Moot point. I'm never getting married, Charlotte." When she raised her eyebrows and gestured to the chapel in front of them, he laughed. "This is the only exception to that rule. *You're* the only exception to that rule. So there's nothing to worry about. Now if that's your only objection, we'd better get going. We're already five minutes late, and I have a feeling there'll be another couple coming right behind us. Let's get married."

She stared at him for a minute. Then she drew in a long deep breath and nodded.

"All right. Fine. I give up. Let's go get married. Sort of."

He grinned. "Now you're talking."

Chapter Nine

"Stand right here, honey." The middle-aged woman who'd introduced herself as Coral Mayler nudged Charlotte into position. "You'll show up better in the pictures, not that you're going to need much help with that. You make a pretty bride. Now," she lowered her voice to a whisper, "if you want, you can turn just a little bit to the side. I'll tell Mel to take only a headshot, so your tummy ain't in the picture. That's up to you."

"This is fine, thanks."

"The groom stands right here, opposite. There you go." Coral gave Logan's shirt collar a motherly tweak. "Ain't you a handsome one? Y'all make a real nice couple. You sure you don't want any organ music? That's free of charge, and it adds a real fancy touch."

"Just the ceremony," Charlotte said.

Coral looked disappointed, but she nodded. "Wait here, and I'll get my husband. He's the one who does the vows." She scurried through a door at the back of the tiny chapel. "Mel!" They heard her calling. "They're ready!"

Charlotte's heartbeat picked up. Was *she* ready? She didn't know.

None of this felt real. She clamped her fingers around

the damp stems of her pretty bouquet and bit down hard on her lower lip. She felt like she was trapped in some sort of nonsense dream. When she'd left Ruby's this morning, she was going out for pancakes. Now she and Logan were about to get legally married in this strange little place.

She glanced around the chapel. It was small and simple, with stained board walls and a few dusty decorations. It was a far cry from the stately Savannah church where she'd married Dylan with every bit of pomp and circumstance Elizabeth could arrange. She remembered how the echoing church had smelled that summer evening—of beeswax candles and masses of chilled flowers. She recalled the weighty drag of her cathedral train. At Elizabeth's insistence, Charlotte had worn her mother-in-law's wedding gown. The dress had consisted of acres of heavy satin that Charlotte had been strictly forbidden to alter in any way.

She hadn't wanted to cause a rift with her new mother-in-law, and it was already apparent that disagreeing with Elizabeth wouldn't be well received. But Charlotte had hated that dress with a passion. She'd felt smothered in it.

Looking back, it had been an excellent preview of things to come.

"You okay?" Logan murmured. She glanced at him, but before she could answer, heavy footsteps pounded up the hidden hallway.

"If I've told you once, I've told you a hundred times, Mel. Don't eat onions on days we got weddings stacked up one after the other. Go brush your teeth so you don't knock this poor young couple flat out on the floor." She poked her head through the door. "It'll be just another minute, sweeties." Then she disappeared again.

Charlotte looked up at Logan. As the two of them sputtered into laughter, her heart lifted and lightened.

It was all right. This was nothing like her wedding to

Dylan. She was with Logan now. And when she was with him, everything was always all right.

Mel turned out to be a kindly-looking balding man who smelled of mint toothpaste and onions. He waited as Coral and a younger woman with bright yellow rubber cleaning gloves on her hands settled in seats, prepared to witness the ceremony. His glance dipped briefly to Charlotte's obviously pregnant tummy, but his kind expression never changed. He adjusted his suit jacket over his own chubby stomach, nodded solemnly and intoned, "Dearly beloved."

Charlotte's first wedding had taken a full hour, and that was just for the ceremony. This one was over in less than ten minutes. The only thing that felt the same was her sense of detached disbelief as Logan repeated the traditional vows and her own voice echoed them. She felt the slide of the gold band over her finger, the unfamiliar smoothness so different from her earlier one, which had bristled with diamonds.

"You may kiss the bride," Mel announced.

Logan winked and leaned down.

She knew he was simply going to brush his lips over hers. She knew that, and she knew this was Logan, who would never hurt her or any other woman, not in a million years.

But still, as he neared her, she flinched backward. She couldn't help it.

As Logan pulled back, his gaze narrowed, flicking over her face with a surprise that deepened into concern.

Thankfully Coral picked that very moment to produce a deafening peal from the overamplified organ in the corner of the room, having apparently overruled their refusal of music. The "Wedding March" played merrily as the two of them walked arm in arm down the short aisle.

They had to pause for the last of the paperwork, but in

no time they were stepping outside, sidestepping another couple on their way in.

As soon as they were safely away from the chapel, Logan stopped and looked at her. "You okay?"

"Yes," she assured him. "This seems a little weird, I guess. What about you? Feel any different?"

He smiled, but he didn't answer the question. "Now that the deed's done, I'd better call Maggie and let her know. She can break the news to Ruby, and by the time we make it home, maybe everything will have tuned down to a dull roar."

He'd opened the truck door for her, but she hesitated, looking at him in alarm. "Your family doesn't know about this? Not even Ruby?"

She'd assumed Ruby would have been in on it. It had even crossed her mind that Ruby might have planted the idea in Logan's head.

"No, she has no idea. I figured we'd better talk it over first and come to a decision." He looked uncomfortable. "If I'd suggested to Ruby that you and I were thinking about getting married…well. You can imagine how she'd have reacted. We'd never have been allowed to slip off here by ourselves, for one thing. She'd have insisted on coming along and bringing the whole family with her."

"Even though it's not a real marriage? We *are* going to make that clear, right?"

"Of course." He shot her a look, reminding her who she was talking to. "The thing is, I'm not sure Ruby's going to see the difference, so you'd better be prepared for that."

She felt herself tensing up. "Oh, boy."

"Don't worry. She'll understand. Eventually. I'll go make the call now. Give me just a minute. Okay?" He waited for her nod, then stepped away from the truck and raised his phone to his ear.

She watched from her seat, trying to read his sister's reaction from the set of his shoulders. Whatever was being said took a while, and when he finally finished talking and turned back toward the truck, he looked frustrated.

"I'm guessing that didn't go too well," she said when he climbed in the driver's seat.

"About like you'd expect. Maggie went from shocked to thrilled to irritated in about twenty seconds."

"Uh-oh."

"It's not like that," he said quickly. "She's not mad about us getting married, although she did point out that running off to get married without telling anybody ahead of time was a chicken thing to do. She didn't get short with me until I said the word *temporary*. Apparently, she'd just as soon keep you as a sister-in-law. She agreed to tell Ruby and the rest of them, but only if I promised to bring you by the farmhouse as soon as we get back to Cedar Ridge." He looked pained. "You know what that means."

"What?"

"There's going to be a family party. I could practically hear Maggie planning what kind of cake she was going to bake. Sorry, Charlotte. I tried to get it across that we didn't want a fuss, that this wasn't that kind of thing, but Maggie's good at tuning you out when you're telling her something she doesn't want to hear."

"She's not the only one," Charlotte said pointedly. "They're throwing us a party?"

"I know. I'm sorry, but you know how my family can be."

Yes, she did. That was what had her stomach knotting up.

Logan's siblings were closer than any family she'd ever known, and they all cared deeply about each other. And because each of them had come from a hard situation, they took marriage and family very seriously.

How would they react to this?

This whole thing had happened so fast, and she'd been focused on what it would mean for her and the baby. She hadn't considered how Logan's family might feel about him entering into an arrangement like this. She should have.

For one thing, no matter how carefully they explained this to Ruby, she'd have a hard time understanding that this marriage wasn't for real. And once she did, she certainly wouldn't approve. She was going to be upset, and by the end of it, she'd probably blame Charlotte.

That sounded familiar. Great. Now Charlotte had two mothers-in-law who disapproved of her. She shuddered.

"You all right?"

Her little shiver hadn't gone unnoticed. She glanced sideways at Logan, feeling a tiny quirk of annoyance. How many times had he asked her some version of that question today? Was he planning to hover over her and make a fuss every time she winced?

That was going to get irritating.

"I'm fine," she said shortly. "Just tired. It's been an intense day."

"Oh." He looked concerned. "Yeah, I guess it has been. Want to try to grab a nap? We have a couple hours' drive ahead of us."

She nodded and closed her eyes, leaning her head against the cool smoothness of the truck's window. And she kept them closed even though she knew she wasn't going to be able to quiet her mind enough to sleep. She was too rattled by the idea of having to face Logan's family as his *sort-of* wife.

She didn't think she could stand having another family reject her—especially not Logan's. She'd always felt so at home with them, so welcomed and loved. She'd often secretly wished they were *her* family, too.

Now they were—legally anyway. And yet she'd never felt more like an outsider than she did right now.

She sighed softly. This wasn't turning out so differently than her first wedding day, after all.

It was nearly dusk by the time they turned onto the dirt drive leading up to Ruby's farmhouse. Logan cast a concerned look at Charlotte.

She wasn't sleeping, although she'd pretended to be most of the drive back from Tennessee. He was worried about her.

He'd insisted on stopping at a steakhouse just inside the Georgia line, sure that she needed to eat something. She'd only picked at her food, though, and that had worried him more.

"Do you want to order something else?" he'd asked. "Maybe some fries for the road?"

She'd shaken her head. "No thanks."

"You've barely eaten anything, Charlotte." Mama B had packed their pancakes up in a to-go box, but she'd only nibbled at hers.

"Because I'm not hungry," she'd said sharply.

He'd dropped the subject. Once they were back on the road, she'd flashed him a guilty look.

"I didn't mean to snap at you. I'm tired. And…a little worried about facing your family."

He'd gathered that much. He just hadn't figured out why.

Sure, his family would have plenty to say about this— and they'd say it loudly. There was no way around that. There was also absolutely no telling how many of them would be at Ruby's house. Maggie lived in town, so she was a sure thing. His brother Ryder and sister Torey were within driving distance, so them, too, probably. Nick and Jina were iffier because they lived farther away, but he'd be hearing from them.

His family was closer than most. Each of them had gone without family long enough to appreciate it when they finally got one. They looked after Ruby and each other. When one of them had a problem, they all did. And when one of them celebrated a milestone, they all converged.

A marriage, even one like this, would be considered a milestone. Every one of his siblings would have an opinion about what he'd done, and most of them would be angry that he'd done it without talking it over with them first. Ruby would, too.

But any hard feelings they had would be directed his way. They'd never be unkind to Charlotte. And if for some reason they did cross that line, they'd answer to him.

Logan realized he was scowling at the road. He relaxed and shook his head.

Where had all that come from?

He glanced over at Charlotte. She looked pale, and she was massaging her temples with one hand. He suddenly noticed a thin white scar running along her hairline that hadn't been there back in high school.

He recalled that telling flinch when he'd leaned down to kiss her in the chapel, and his gut tightened.

Family or not, he and Charlotte needed to have a talk.

They'd reached the fork in the drive, and on impulse he turned the truck to the steeper incline leading up to the cabin. Charlotte peeked through her fingers and frowned.

"Where are we going?"

"To the cabin."

"But your family—"

"Can wait."

The old cabin rested peacefully in its clearing, as a

spectacular sunset shot pink-and-gold streaks across the sky. As Logan helped Charlotte up to the porch, he heard the faint echo of voices drifting up from the farm. Sound carried up here. Not well enough for him to recognize the person talking, but he could guess. The crowd was gathering at Ruby's.

He glanced at Charlotte who was gazing up at the colorful sky. Beauty always soothed her, and her expression was already more relaxed than it had been. He'd intended to talk inside, but instead he pointed toward the wooden swing.

"Have a seat. I'll be right back."

When he came back out, she was still studying the fading sunset.

"Here." He held out the travel mug he'd fixed for her back in the kitchen. "I know you're not feeling much like eating, but you need to have something. Skipping meals can't be good for you in your condition."

She didn't look happy, but she didn't disagree with him. "What is it?"

"Taste it and see."

When she put the mug up to her mouth, her eyebrows lifted. "Chocolate milk? What are we? Four?"

"Hey, it's milk," he pointed out. "That's healthy. And I made it with that powder mix we used to like. Remember? The one in the pink box? It's good."

"That's because it's almost pure sugar." A smile tickled around her mouth, and she took another sip. Then a third. He counted that a win. "I can't believe you still drink this stuff."

He didn't, usually. He'd noticed the familiar tub at the grocery. His mind had already been stuck on Charlotte, so he'd tossed it into his cart on impulse. Then he'd been too embarrassed to truck it along to Ruby's, so he'd stashed it in his kitchen instead. "See the kind of things you learn about a guy when you marry him?"

She rolled her eyes at his joke, but she took another sip.

"I'm sorry if I've gotten on your nerves today, fussing over you too much. I've never had a pregnant wife before, so I'm kind of clueless here. If you have any tips, I'm all ears."

She made a face at him. "I actually do have one."

"Lay it on me."

"For future reference, if I'm not okay, I'll let you know. You don't have to ask me every five minutes."

He laughed. "I'll try to remember that. But when I slip up—and you'll notice that's a when, not an if—just remind me."

"Fair enough." She pushed a foot against the floor to set the swing swaying and changed the subject. "It sure is quiet up here."

Right on cue, a dim shout echoed up from the farm—Torey, unless he missed his guess. Charlotte glanced in that direction and frowned.

"Yeah, they're down there." He settled on the swing beside her. "We'll go meet them in a little while, but I thought we'd better talk first."

"About what?"

"About how we're planning to handle all this, for starters. We haven't really hashed it all out yet, and my family's going to ask. Like, where are we going to live?"

She looked uncomfortable. "Oh."

"What about here?"

"Both of us?"

"Well, yes." He waited. "You like the cabin, and it just makes more sense. My apartment's only got the one bedroom, but there are two up here. You can take the bigger one, and we can put a crib in there for the baby once he gets here."

"You think we need to live together?"

"Yeah, Charlotte, I do. We can double-check it with Eric, if you want. I plan to call him in anyway, to let him know about this. But I'm pretty sure he's going to say we'll need to live together if we want the marriage to carry any weight in a legal fight."

Her grip had tightened on the mug, but she nodded. "You're probably right. Elizabeth won't take this well. She'll have her lawyer look for loopholes, anything she can use against me. If we're not living together, she'll find out." She sighed. "I should talk to Eric myself. I know how Elizabeth thinks, and I can guess the kinds of things she'll try."

"That's a good idea." He hesitated. "And Charlotte? I think you should tell him about Dylan, too."

She winced. "I know."

"I understand it won't be easy, but I think it's important that he know what was happening to you. How's it's affected you." He hesitated, then went on, "Like back at the chapel when I started to kiss you…it made you nervous." He felt her shrinking away from him, but he needed to know. "Is that because of Dylan, too?"

She stood up quickly, making the swing bounce. "I'd like to freshen up, before we go to Ruby's."

"Sure." He stood and opened the door, then closed it gently behind her.

She didn't have to run away. He wouldn't ask any more questions. He didn't need to. He already had his answer.

And it made him sick to his stomach.

He punched in Eric's number on the phone and explained to his astonished friend the events of his day.

"Wow," the attorney said. "I don't know what else to say except…wow."

"Charlotte needs to talk to you. It won't be an easy conversation for her. I don't know if she'll let me come along or not, but either way, you'll need to go slow and let her take the lead."

His friend blew out a sigh. "Not the first time I've dealt with something like this, I'm sorry to say. I won't push her."

"Good. I'll give her your number and she'll call you to set up an appointment. In the meantime, there's something else I'd like you to do for me."

"Shoot."

"Tell Findlay to give Elizabeth Tremaine a message. Tell him Charlotte and I are a team now. What happens to her happens to me, and I don't react well to being bullied."

There was snort from the other end of the line. "That's the understatement of the year. I'll make that clear, but I doubt it'll do much good. Talk's cheap with a guy like Findlay. If we want him to take us seriously, we're going to have to do a lot more than threaten."

"I'm not threatening. I'm promising. You tell Findlay I don't care how many cases he's got under his belt, this is one he's not going to win. Dylan Tremaine was a wife-beating coward, and his mother gets custody of Charlotte's baby over my dead body."

"Understood. Although I'll reword that part in the paperwork."

"I don't care how you word it, Eric. Just make sure they understand it."

Logan ended the call and turned to find Charlotte standing in the doorway.

"That," she said, "is not going to go over well." She shook her head at him, but he didn't care. He could see a hint of the old spark shining in her eyes.

"Probably not. But wouldn't you like to be a fly on the wall when Findlay gives Elizabeth that message?"

"You know what?" Charlotte's lips tipped up. "I would."

"So would I." He closed the gap between them and took her right hand in his, gently sliding her mother's class ring off her finger.

He handed it to her. "You can put this away. Like I told Eric, we're officially a team now, you and me, and whatever trouble comes, we'll get through it together." Another shout drifted dimly up the mountain, and he sighed. "Speaking of trouble. Come on, Mrs. Carter. I think it's time to face up to the family."

Chapter Ten

Charlotte had forgotten how loud Logan's family could be.

By nine o'clock that night, Ruby's kitchen was crammed with her kids, all trying to adjust to the curveball they'd been tossed. And eating cake, of course, because Maggie Hamilton never went anywhere without bringing a treat.

Tonight, it was an elaborate two-tiered production that must have taken her hours to put together. Decorated lavishly with pink sugar flowers and tiny blue baby shoes, the cake seemed to be some sort of joyful, confusing crossover celebrating both motherhood and weddings.

The confusing part was appropriate, since Logan's family was openly befuddled by his sudden marriage and impending stepfatherhood. Just as he'd predicted, his brothers and sisters had descended on Ruby's farmhouse with noisy astonishment, demanding explanations.

According to Ruby, Maggie had arrived first with her husband, Neil, and their two children, breaking the news of the marriage to her foster mother. She'd already called her siblings, so Ryder had driven up not long after. Right now he was alternating *what were you two thinking* remarks with complaints about the condition of Ruby's driveway.

According to Logan, hotshot salesman Ryder Montgomery could sell snow cones in a blizzard, but so far he'd failed to convince his foster mom to let him shoulder the expense of having her driveway paved.

Middle sister Torey had arrived just after Ryder. Charlotte remembered her as the prickliest of Logan's sisters, brilliant and intensely loyal to her foster family. Now a computer security specialist, Torey stayed quieter than the others, a wary glint in her eyes whenever she looked in Charlotte's direction. Although too far away to drive in on such short notice, the remaining two siblings, Jina and Nick, had been included via separate video chats using Ryder's high-powered phone.

Maggie's husband, Neil, had sent Charlotte several sympathetic glances, and when he'd passed by on his way to the refrigerator, he'd murmured, "I know how it feels to be the new kid on the block with this bunch. Trust me—once the dust settles, things will be fine."

She'd smiled bravely back at him, but she wasn't so sure. Maggie and Neil had married for love and planned to stay together forever. Her situation with Logan wasn't the same thing at all.

She hoped everyone understood that. Especially Ruby.

She watched the older woman feeding Maggie's adopted son Oliver a bite of cake and laughing at his rapt expression. Maybe it was coincidence, but the baby kicked in Charlotte's womb, almost as if he wished he could be a part of this family celebration, too.

He'd been making himself felt all day, in one way or another—a good reminder that she wasn't the only one impacted by everything that had happened today.

When she winced, Logan frowned and leaned over.

"I won't ask. But I'll remind you that you said you'd let me know if you aren't okay."

"I'm fine."

He looked unconvinced. "It's been a long day. Maybe you should go ahead and pack up whatever you'll need tonight at the cabin. We'll be leaving pretty soon."

Her stomach fluttered at the thought. It was so strange, realizing that—for now, anyway—her home would be at the cabin with Logan. "Okay."

"Need any help?" When she shook her head, he added, "All right, but humor me and don't try to carry out your suitcase. If you're anything like my sisters, a night's worth of girly stuff is going to weigh a ton. Just get it ready and I'll take it to the truck."

She managed a smile. "You've got a deal."

Grateful for a chance to escape for a few minutes, she slipped from the room. When she shut the sturdy bedroom door behind herself, she felt a rush of guilty relief.

She didn't blame Logan's family for being bewildered and unsure about all this. She felt the same way, and that had made facing them tonight feel even more overwhelming. She was thankful for the break.

She opened her suitcase and began the process of packing up her belongings. She was nearly finished when there was a soft knock on the door.

"Not quite done, Logan. Give me another minute?"

"It's me, honey." The door opened a crack, and Ruby poked her head in. "I thought maybe you and me should have ourselves a little talk."

"All right." This was what she'd been dreading most, but she might as well get it over with. "Come on in."

Ruby slipped inside, then shut the door firmly. "We won't have long, I expect. If I stay gone longer than ten minutes, one of 'em comes looking for me. I should never have told the kids about those sinking spells I had this past summer. It's got 'em all in a wad. I love them to pieces, but they'll drive a body distracted with their hovering."

In spite of her nerves, Charlotte smiled. "I know just what you mean."

"I'm sure you do. Logan's the worst of the lot of them. He means well, of course, and he can't help it. It's who he is. God made that boy to take care of people. Looking after folks is the call on Logan's life, you could say. I expect that's why—"

"—why he married me," Charlotte finished. "Yes, I'm sure you're right."

Ruby raised an eyebrow. "I was going to say, that's why he went into law enforcement." She sat on the bed and patted the spread. "Have a seat, honey." When Charlotte had settled beside her, she smiled. "Truth is, I think my boy had other reasons for marrying you. Reasons he ain't even fully aware of yet himself."

Charlotte felt a pinprick of alarm. She wasn't sure exactly how she could explain this, but she had to try. "Logan's helping me out of a tough situation, Ruby. It's the most unselfish thing anybody has ever done for me, and I'll be grateful to him for the rest of my life. But we've both been clear with each other. This marriage is just for legal reasons, and it's temporary. Logan and I are friends, and we're planning to stay that way. Just friends." She took the woman's bony hand in hers. "I don't want you to be upset, but I need to make sure you understand right from the start. We aren't like Maggie and Neil."

Ruby gave her fingers a squeeze. "'Course you aren't. No two couples are ever alike. But you ain't as different as you might think. You and Logan both care about what happens with this little one here." Gently, Ruby laid her free hand on Charlotte's swollen middle. "Maggie and Neil started off caring about Oliver. It took 'em a while to start caring about each other, but that came along in God's good time. You and Logan got a head start on that. You care about each other already."

"We do, but not in the same way. I want to be really clear because I know how long you've been praying for Logan to find somebody and settle down."

"You're right, honey. I have been praying, and praying's a dangerous business. God's got odd ways of answering sometimes, and He ain't above using trouble to scoot us along in the right direction." The old woman smiled. "He's got a real interesting sense of humor, too, I've noticed. So you two can say whatever you want, but I see the Lord's fingerprints all over this marriage. May take some time for you to see that for yourselves, but I got faith it'll happen by and by."

"Ruby, Logan and I—"

"I know," she interrupted. "You're just friends. I heard you the first time, and I won't fuss about it with you. It ain't a good idea to argue with a pregnant woman. The baby's liable to end up with colic. But I'll say this much. Being good friends who help each other and care about each other? That don't sound like such a bad start for a marriage to me. Does it to you?"

Well, no, it didn't. But that was beside the point. As she tried to figure out a better way to get that across to Ruby, a contraction tightened the muscles around Charlotte's middle, and she winced.

Ruby frowned. "You paining, honey?"

"It's just Braxton Hicks. I get them off and on, especially when I'm feeling stressed. They aren't coming regularly, so it's nothing to worry about."

"My Maggie had those, too." The older woman's face relaxed. "False labor, they call it. Even so, I don't think it's a good idea for you to sit up there in that cabin by your lonesome all day while Logan's at work. Besides, we got that quilt to finish. We'd best get to it before this baby comes along, 'cause we won't have near so much time to work on it then. Tell you what, why don't you plan on spending your days over here with me, same as we did before?"

So Ruby wasn't going to reject her after all. Charlotte smiled with relief. "I'd like that." Then she frowned as a suspicion dawned. "Wait a minute. Did Logan ask you to invite me over?"

Ruby cackled and patted Charlotte's arm. "No, he didn't, but I guarantee he will before you two leave this farm tonight. Seems you know that husband of yours mighty well already, honey." The older woman pushed off the bed. "Now, you're looking tired. I'll go tell him you're about ready to go home. Okay?"

Charlotte nodded, but her mind lingered on what Ruby had said.

Her husband. For the second time in her life, she was someone's wife.

This morning she'd walked out of this cozy room on her way to have breakfast with her best friend, and now, in just a few minutes, she was leaving it to go home *with her husband*.

She bit her lip as another Braxton Hicks clamped around her middle. What on earth had she gotten herself into?

On his first morning as a married man, Logan stood at the cabin window watching the sunrise and draining his second mug of strong, black coffee. It wouldn't be his last, because he hadn't slept much. He'd been too revved up on adrenaline to sleep, and his brain had been in overdrive.

Not surprising. He'd gone from single to married-about-to-be-a-father in one day. That was enough to keep any man awake.

But the changes in his life went even deeper than that.

He hadn't fully realized how deep until he'd walked into Ruby's last night. Until he'd met his mom's eyes, seen the stunned expressions on the faces of his sisters and brothers and heard the concern in their careful questions.

Until he'd felt himself tensing up prepared to do battle on Charlotte's behalf if any of them had stepped out of line.

That alone was a big red flag. He'd never even considered squaring off against his family before. Not for anybody.

Thankfully, everybody had behaved themselves. As close as they'd become over the years, his brothers and sisters still toed careful lines with each other. They might not always agree, but they guarded each others' bruised hearts and loved each other fiercely.

And yet, yesterday he'd gone off and gotten married without giving them a heads-up. That had hurt them. He'd seen that. And it had caused a little rift between them. The rift would heal—he'd make sure of it. But no matter how he explained it, they hadn't understood why he'd have made such a big decision without talking to them about it—and the truth was, neither did he.

Nobody in the world trumped Logan's family in his heart. At least, nobody ever had. But somehow, now, Charlotte did. He couldn't begin to explain that to them. He couldn't even explain it to himself. But it was so.

And that right there waved another red flag. His feelings for Charlotte had crossed a line somewhere without him noticing.

He'd tried to figure out when that had happened. Maybe it had started when she'd made Ruby drive her to this cabin in the middle of the night, worried over him. Something had shifted inside him when he'd seen her cuddled on the couch, holding one of his dirty shirts against her face. Before that, Charlotte had been his friend, a good friend, one that he cared about deeply, but still, a friend. But somewhere between that moment and this one, she and her unborn baby had become his number one priority.

Last night, after she'd gone to bed, he'd dropped down on the couch and rolled the plain gold ring around on his finger. Charlotte was officially under his protection now, legally, morally and every other way that counted in this world. If anybody tried to hurt her, they'd have to get past him first.

For the first time, he'd asked himself why getting to that point had mattered enough to him that he was willing to upend his whole life and offend his family over it.

He still wasn't sure of the answer to that, but he didn't have to be Einstein to know he was skirting some dangerous heart territory. Given the situation they were in now, that wasn't good.

The only way this worked was if he kept his feelings strictly in the friendship zone. That's what he'd promised Charlotte, and that's what he had to do.

He glanced at his watch. He needed to get to work, but he didn't want to wake Charlotte, and he didn't want to leave her without saying goodbye. He looked at the closed bedroom door and considered his options.

Finally he scrawled her a note. *Ruby's expecting you at the farm today. Path's kind of rocky, so when you're ready, take the truck and drive over.* He hesitated for a minute. How should he sign it? Finally he settled on, *Call my cell or the office if you need anything.* Another long hesitation before he finally scrawled *Always, Logan.* He anchored the note on the kitchen table with his truck keys before heading out the door.

One thing about living in a small town, everyone knew your business almost as soon as you did. Logan figured the news of the wedding would have made the rounds quicker than a summer cold, and he was right.

Marla jumped up the minute he walked into the office, her face alight with excitement. "Here comes the groom! You sure had an eventful day yesterday, Sheriff!"

He shot her a discouraging look. "Yes, I did. But I'm not planning to talk about my personal life at work. Put the word out. Post it on the bulletin board if you have to, but make sure everybody gets the message."

Her face fell. "But…we all thought maybe we should have a party or something. I mean, this kind of thing doesn't happen every day."

"Marla."

She sighed. "Fine." She picked up a gift bag from her desk and held it out. "Here. Congratulations. I guess."

"Thank you."

"It's not for you. Fresh coffee's in the break room." She plopped down at the radio and ignored him.

The break room was blessedly empty, so he paused to grab a cup of coffee before heading for his office. As he waited for his computer to power up, he studied the gift bag sitting on his desk.

Curious, he pulled the tuft of tissue paper out of the top and unfolded a tiny outfit, something Maggie called a onesie. This one had a badge on the front and the numbers 10-41.

Logan grinned. That meant *beginning tour of duty*.

Cute.

When he went to stuff it back into the bag, his eye caught on the words printed on the back.

Behave Yourself! My Daddy's the Sheriff.

He sat there for a minute staring at the tiny thing, both his coffee and the humming computer forgotten.

This was for real. In a few weeks, he was going to be somebody's daddy. Well, a stepdaddy. But still.

That was a really, really big deal.

"Told you it wasn't for you."

Marla was standing in the doorway.

"Thank you." He dropped it in the bag and tucked the tissue back into place. "It's really cute."

"Hard to find baby stuff that isn't. Listen, I've got a man out there asking to see you."

"Oh?" He set the gift bag on the bookshelf behind him, out of sight. He'd never be able to focus on work with it in his line of vision. "Who is it?"

"Some lawyer." She leaned over and put a card on his desk.

Logan had started tapping computer keys, bringing up the day's schedule. He finished that before glancing at the card.

Then he looked again.

"Send him in. Then call Eric Dawson and see if he can come down here."

"Yes, sir." Marla paused, frowning. "Something wrong, Sheriff?"

"Nothing I can't handle."

Marla nodded and left. Alone in his office, Logan said a silent, fierce prayer. Then he pushed his chair away from the desk and stood.

If trouble had come calling, he planned to meet it on his feet—and head-on.

Trouble—in the form of Lou Findlay—strode through the door five minutes later. The man looked like exactly what he was—a high-priced attorney. Smelled like one, too. The cologne he wore was both expensive and over-powering. Logan suspected it matched the man's person-ality perfectly.

"Mr. Findlay." He offered the man his hand and felt an immature satisfaction when the guy winced at his grip. "Have a seat."

The lawyer did, subtly angling the chair so that his back was against the window. "Thank you, Sheriff. I appreciate your being willing to talk to me on such short notice. I'm sure you're a busy man, so I won't take up much of your time."

Logan leaned back in his own chair and lifted an eyebrow. "I expect you're a busy man, too, Mr. Findlay. And here you've driven all the way up here from Savannah, just for a talk. Couldn't you have handled that just as well over the phone?"

The other man chuckled. "I find some things are better handled face-to-face. Don't you?"

"Some things are," Logan agreed. Then he waited. Silence was a valuable tool. People didn't like it much, and it tended to throw them off-balance.

Findlay seemed perfectly comfortable with it, though. He let it stretch out awhile before continuing. "I received a phone call from an attorney friend of yours late yesterday evening. He gave me to understand congratulations are in order."

"That why you've driven all this way? To congratulate me?"

Another light laugh. "I wish it were that simple. No, Sheriff Carter, I'm afraid I've come here to pass along some important information from my client, Elizabeth Tremaine. Information we think you'll find...instructive."

The atmosphere in the room went stiff and still. "You came here to warn me, you mean. About what?"

"Well, first of all, you should know that, although the Tremaines are a financially secure family, Charlotte Tremaine has no monetary assets of her own. In fact, her late husband left her in quite a regrettable position." The lawyer steepled his fingers together. "Just in case you were under any misapprehension there."

"I was not. Next?"

"Mrs. Tremaine will be glad to hear that. She's concerned that you might have been misled. She's well aware that their daughter-in-law has been under a great deal of stress since Dylan's death. That, and the pregnancy, along with Charlotte's history of mental instability—"

"Charlotte's not mentally unstable."

"I'm afraid that's well-documented. Quite well-documented, actually, by some very reputable professionals."

"If these professionals have seen Charlotte as a patient, that information would be confidential. Wouldn't it?"

The lawyer blinked. Score. "I didn't say they'd seen her in that capacity. Their observations have been…informal."

"In other words, they're friends of Mrs. Tremaine who are willing to lie."

The lawyer released a long-suffering sigh. "Either way, it's going to come out in court. As will your own history, which, as you know, is rather…colorful."

"Excuse me?"

"Oh, no disrespect intended. Quite the contrary. You've cleaned yourself up very well. Made something of yourself. You've even been elected sheriff. No mean feat for somebody with a career criminal for a father." The attorney flicked something off his pants leg. "How many times has he been in jail? Eight, I think? But I might have missed a couple of short stints."

"That's my father's history. Not mine."

"I see. Have you been in touch with your father lately? He's not currently incarcerated, I believe. Do you have any idea what he's been doing?"

"No, and I don't care." Logan narrowed his eyes. "Look,

Findlay. Maybe you make your living bandying innuendos and threats around. I don't, and I have some real work to do. Why don't you just say what you've come here to say?"

"All right. Man to man, here's the truth of it. Marriage or not, this custody case isn't going Charlotte's way."

"It already has. You wouldn't have driven all the way down here if it hadn't."

"My client's concerned about her daughter-in-law and her unborn grandson. Given your personal family history, understandably so. She's worried you're taking advantage of a woman who's on the brink of a nervous breakdown, and who requires the kind of medical attention and care that my client can easily afford."

"You can tell Elizabeth Tremaine that Charlotte's not her daughter-in-law anymore. She's my wife. Whatever she needs I'll provide." He stood. "If that's all you have to say, I think we're done here."

Findlay stayed in his chair. "There's just one more thing. My client is concerned about Charlotte, but, of course, she's an adult who has the right to make her own decisions. Even when they appear…" the man's gaze flicked over Logan, "questionable," he finished smoothly.

Logan gritted his teeth. "But?"

"But the child she's carrying is a Tremaine. An only son's only son. My client's one chance for a grandchild. She's not going to back away from this."

"Then she's about to waste an awful lot of time and money."

"Which she has to waste. Face it. You're outgunned here, Sheriff. But if Charlotte gives in gracefully, then perhaps a generous visitation schedule could be arranged. Otherwise, I'm afraid this could end very unpleasantly."

"Get out."

"Sheriff?" He glanced over to find Marla back in the

doorway, waving a scrap of paper. "I have an important message for you."

Probably a message saying Eric was tied up and couldn't come by. "It doesn't matter now. Mr. Findlay was just leaving."

The attorney offered another oily smile as he rose to his feet. "Talk things over with your…wife. Then give me a call. Oh, and best wishes on that upcoming election." He winked. "From what I hear you have a substantial lead right now, but voters can surprise you."

He edged through the doorway, past Marla who stared after him wide-eyed.

She glanced back at Logan. "That guy seems like a piece of work."

"He is. About that message, just shoot Eric an email and let him know Findlay came by. Tell him I'll give him a call later and fill him in on the details."

"Oh!" Marla's expression shifted. "I can't believe I'm just standing here! Eric's secretary said he was in court this morning. I couldn't get hold of him. The message is from Ruby. She's taking Charlotte to the hospital. Her water broke."

Chapter Eleven

"They're going to take real good care of you here." Ruby walked alongside the wheelchair, keeping a comforting hand on Charlotte's shoulder as the nurse rolled her to the maternity ward. "This might be a small hospital, but it's a good one."

"I'm sure it is."

That was a polite fib. She wasn't sure at all. This tiny place seemed a world away from the top-notch facility in Savannah, and she hadn't even met the doctor who'd be delivering her baby.

Worst of all, her baby was coming early. That was exactly what Dr. Edwards had cautioned her about, and she wasn't sure what sort of problems it might create. All of those things together were making her awfully nervous.

"Hey!"

A familiar, deep voice echoed down the corridor, causing her to go limp with relief.

Logan.

"Stop," she said to the nurse. "Stop please. That's—" she paused, and then managed "—my husband."

The nurse didn't seem to need any introductions. She beamed at Logan as he caught up with them. "Hi, Sheriff!"

"Hi, Emily." He flashed a quick smile, before focusing his attention on Charlotte. "I got here as quick as I could. How are you doing?"

"That's what we're about to find out," the nurse said cheerfully. "Come on, everybody. We need to get her to a room and get this party started."

Logan took her hand—the one that wore his simple ring—in his own. "Emily, how about you put her in that corner room? Anybody in there?"

"Nope. We're quiet today. She'll be the only one on the floor unless Allie Calvert goes into labor. She's a week past due."

"Any room's fine." Charlotte cast an apprehensive look at the nurse. "I don't want to be any trouble."

"It's no trouble, sweetie, and the sheriff knows what he's talking about. That's the nicest room on the whole floor. Farthest from the elevators, but closest to the nursery and the nurses' station."

"Who's working today?" Logan asked in a low voice. "I want her assigned the best nurse on the staff. You'll know who that is, Emily, and that's the one we want."

"Relax, cowboy. I'll see to her myself until shift change. Then I'll hand her over to Melissa. You'll love her," she promised Charlotte. "All our mothers do."

"I'm sure all the nurses are good," Charlotte said, but Logan frowned.

"Melissa who?"

"Logan," Charlotte protested.

"That'll be Melissa Evans," Ruby interrupted. "Johnny and Karen's girl. You know her, son. She was on duty when Maggie's Gracie was born. Tall girl with real pretty curly hair. She went to school with our Torey."

"Yeah, I remember her. She knows her stuff?"

"All our people know their stuff, but in my opinion,

she's the best OB-GYN nurse we have on staff." Emily wheeled Charlotte into a spacious room, decorated in soothing rose tones. "Melissa could deliver that baby herself if the doc doesn't make it back from the golf course in time."

Logan looked alarmed. "He's playing golf? Have you called him yet?"

"I will as soon as I've completed the exam." When Logan started to protest, Emily clucked her tongue. "I've been patient, 'cause you're a new daddy and all that. But now you're starting to get on my nerves. Believe it or not, Sheriff, this isn't the first baby we've delivered. We have our procedures, and you need to back up and let us do our jobs. Now, wait out here while I get your wife all prepped and checked out."

Your wife. Those words were unsettling and comforting at the same time. Charlotte felt as if she were floating on a shifting sea of emotions—nervousness, fear, joy, anticipation.

"I want her to have the best care," Logan was insisting. "The very best."

"No kidding," Emily called over her shoulder as she pushed the door shut with an elbow. "You could've fooled me."

Once they were alone, Charlotte tried to gauge the nurse's reaction to Logan's fussing. She didn't seem annoyed, but sometimes you couldn't tell right away.

Dylan and his mother had always done that—demanded the best of everything wherever they happened to be. They'd been every bit as insistent about it as Logan had been, but a lot less polite. That hadn't always gone over well with people. More than once, Charlotte had been left cleaning up after the Tremaines' arrogance, making apologies to clerks and waiters, smoothing things over.

"Sorry about all that," she offered now.

The nurse was rummaging around, pulling things out of cupboards. "About what, honey?"

"Logan was being pushy."

Emily laughed as she handed Charlotte a folded hospital gown. "Yeah, he was. But so what? He's just excited. I don't know what he's so worried about. He should've known that we'd have given you the VIP treatment whether he asked for it or not." She glanced at Charlotte, looking concerned. "Don't misunderstand me. We take care of all our patients really well. But the sheriff has done so much for so many people that we don't mind going out of our way for him. The way we see it he's one of our own, so you are, too."

She ushered Charlotte into the small bathroom to change. "I'll stand out here, honey. Just holler if you need help."

"Thanks."

When Charlotte opened the door, Emily was waiting to help her to the bed. "Now, I'm going to check you over. This is your first baby, right?"

Charlotte swallowed. "Yes."

Emily leaned down close and looked Charlotte in the eye. "I know you're nervous, sweetie. All first-timers are. But I promise, we're going to look after you and that baby so well even our fussy-pants sheriff will sing our praises for years to come. If you need anything—anything at all, you just let me know and I'll take care of it. Think of me as the sister you never had. Okay?"

In spite of herself, Charlotte smiled. "Okay."

A quick examination later, and Emily opened the door. "You can come in now. Oh, relax. She and the baby are both doing fine," Emily added as Logan made a beeline for Charlotte's bedside. "She's got a long day ahead of her, but she's on her way. I'm going out to call the doctor now."

"Ruby's gone to phone the rest of the family," Logan said after Emily had disappeared. "I'll do my best to keep them corralled, but I'm sure they'll camp out in the waiting room until the baby is born, same as when Gingersnap came along."

"They're coming? Here? All of them?" Charlotte felt a contraction starting, stronger than the ones she'd felt before, and she tightened her grip on the bed rails. "But why? I mean, this isn't the same thing. The baby's not—"

"Not biologically mine? That's not going to matter to my family. None of us are related by blood, remember? That's never made a difference." He paused. "It's not going to make any difference to me, either. I'm here, Charlotte, for both of you. For as long as you want me." He unclenched her hand from the rail and took it into his own. "There. Squeeze as hard as you want. I can take it."

And take it he did. He stayed right beside her, double-checking everything that was done. Emily came close to throwing him out three times, but Logan was in full-blown bodyguard mode, and her good-natured threats made no difference.

Charlotte was pretty sure the nurse was bluffing anyway. Logan, it turned out, was something of a local celebrity.

At the beginning, when her contractions were mild, Charlotte watched him interacting with the hospital staff. Everybody seemed to know him, but that wasn't the surprising thing. Everyone had known the Tremaines, too.

The difference was he knew *them*. All of them, from the janitor and the elderly obstetrician, to the hospital CEO who came down from his office to check on Charlotte personally. Charlotte was puzzled by that until Emily whispered that Logan had worked a bad wreck the man's wife had been involved in a few months back. The sheriff had been first on the scene, and he'd performed CPR until the paramedics had arrived.

There were plenty more stories like that, and she heard them, one after the other.

Logan knew all of their names, asked after their families, brushed aside their thanks for his past help with a practiced ease. He was polite and friendly, but he kept each encounter short, and his focus never left Charlotte for very long. When Melissa came on shift, he pulled her aside for a quiet word. After that, the stream of visitors ceased except for his siblings and Ruby.

She knew he was worried about the baby coming early, in spite of the obstetrician's reassurances. She could read the concern in Logan's face, even though he was doing his best to hide it. Oddly enough, her own nervousness had eased, as the hours passed. There was something soothing about Logan—something calm and solid that held her steady even as her contractions built. When he looked into her eyes and held her hand, all her fears just faded away.

He stayed as long as he could, stepping outside during the exams, quietly without being asked. As soon as they were alone again, he asked how she wanted him to handle this, since their situation wasn't exactly typical. Between contractions, they worked out a plan that seemed reasonable, and even though she could tell that he hated leaving her side, he stuck to his end of the agreement.

When time came for the delivery, he leaned down and brushed a kiss across her damp forehead.

"Right outside, Charlotte," he whispered fiercely. "That's where I'll be. Right outside that door. And I'm sending in reinforcements. Okay?"

She nodded, even though she had no idea what he meant—until Ruby entered the room.

"I'm going to stay right here with you, until the baby's born, honey," the older woman said, her weathered face aglow with excitement. "Maggie wanted the job, but Logan and I overruled her." She paused. "If that's okay with you. Logan said to ask."

Charlotte swallowed hard. "Yes," she managed. "It's okay."

It was a lot more than okay, but she couldn't explain that at the moment. She had more important work to do.

Her son was born forty-five minutes later, a little on the small side, but perfectly healthy and with a lusty cry that made Ruby laugh out loud.

"He's got good lungs, anyhow!"

Charlotte didn't answer. She was too wrapped up in her son's tiny face.

She'd wondered how she'd feel when she saw him—this baby who'd been born out of a marriage she'd longed to escape. But from the first moment Melissa handed him to her, swaddled in a striped hospital blanket, she knew all the time she'd spent worrying had been wasted.

The only thing she felt was love—well, that and an overwhelming desire to show him to Logan.

"Ruby?" she whispered. "Would you ask if Logan can come in now?"

Ruby looked at the nurses who were finishing up their various tasks. "Could you give us a minute?"

They exchanged looks, but nodded. "Sure."

Once they were gone, Ruby turned back to Charlotte. "Honey, what I've got to say I'm going to say quick because there's no way we're keeping my boy out of here for long, whether anybody goes to fetch him or not."

Charlotte cuddled her tiny son closer. Ruby looked worried. "What is it?"

"You know it'd suit me just fine for the two of you to stay married, raise this sweet little fellow together and add more babies to this family. You and Logan have been pretty plain that that's not your plan, but, honey, I need to tell you something. Once my boy walks in that door yonder and sees this baby for the first time, it's going to be all over. This child's going to own him for the rest of his life. And no matter what choices you two make in the future, what's about to happen in this hospital room will never change. Logan will be this baby's father in his heart from here on out." She paused. "You know I'm telling the truth. Don't you?"

"Yes." Charlotte swallowed. "Yes, I know."

"So if you're not good with that, if there's any doubt at all in your head that you can live with sharing this baby for the long haul, then I'm asking you to make that clear to him right up front, right now, loud and clear. It probably won't do one bit of good, but you'll have to try. Because if you don't—" Ruby cleared her throat. "If you don't, honey, one day you're going to break my son's heart into a million pieces."

Charlotte adjusted the baby's position enough to free one hand. She reached out and clasped Ruby's thin arm.

"Ask the nurse to get Logan," she said. "Tell him there's somebody I want him to meet."

Thanks to his choice of profession and his personal history, Logan had an up-close relationship with stressful situations. He liked to think he'd learned to handle them, that he was the kind of man who stayed cool under pressure.

Mostly, he was.

However, being shut out of Charlotte's delivery room and forced to pace the waiting room was taking stress to a whole new level. Every second felt like a year, and by the time an hour had dragged by, his family had quit teasing him. Instead, they were regarding him with a wary amusement and keeping quiet.

Or as quiet as his family could be.

"Have a cookie," Maggie offered when he passed by her seat for the fifth time. Somehow she'd found time to create themed treats to match the occasion. The box she held out was filled with sugar cookies shaped like baby bottles, complete with white icing milk and blue-for-a-boy trimmings. "It'll make you feel better."

He barely glanced at them. "Not hungry."

His sister snapped the lid shut and made an exasperated face. "Logan, believe it or not, the birth of a baby is a happy occasion."

Happy? He wasn't feeling happy. Not yet. Not until he got back in that room and saw for himself that Charlotte was out of pain, that the baby was healthy.

"Leave him be, Mags," his brother-in-law Neil said quietly.

"All right," she muttered. "But remember when I said you were the worst father-to-be worrywart I'd ever met? I take it back. Even you weren't this bad."

"Because I was right there with you. It's a lot harder being out here and not knowing what's going on."

Logan turned and met Neil's eyes. Finally, someone got it. "Thanks."

"You'd better save your strength, Logan." Ryder didn't glance up from the phone he was tapping on. "Postpone some of this freaking-out stuff for later. If you jump the gun and have a heart attack when the kid's being born, what's left for when he starts driving?"

Logan froze in place. That was right. In about fifteen short years, this baby boy would be sliding behind the wheel of an automobile. His mind drifted to all the car wrecks he'd worked involving inexperienced teenaged drivers, and his knees turned to liquid.

"I need to sit down," he mumbled as he dropped into a chair.

"Stop poking the bear, Ryder." Torey looked up from where she was seated cross-legged on the floor. "He's already teetering on the edge. Don't push him over."

With a callousness only a brother could show, Ryder chuckled. "I was just saying. Long road ahead, *Daddy*."

Daddy.

The feelings that had overwhelmed him when he'd pulled out that onesie at the office came flooding back. He was really about to become a kid's dad, and that wasn't something he'd ever planned on. Being an uncle? That was fine. He was good at that.

He might even be great at that.

But being a dad was an entirely different thing.

He'd seen this coming, of course. He'd factored this automatic parenthood before he'd ever brought the idea of marriage up with Charlotte. He'd looked ahead to it and calmly accepted it, with all the responsibilities and commitments that came with that.

Or he thought he had.

But the truth was, now that it came down to it, he realized he had very little idea of how to actually carry out all those responsibilities. He'd never had a dad of his own. He'd had a father, sort of, but that wasn't the same thing.

He understood the difference because he'd grown up studying other kids with their dads. Almost any guy could become a father. That was just a combination of biology and legal status. Not so many men achieved dadhood.

His own father sure hadn't. It had been left to Ruby and a few good-hearted men from their church to fill the gaps that had created in Logan's life. And there had been a lot of gaps. Like the time he'd had to wear a necktie to a school event, and he hadn't had a clue how to tie it.

Not an earth-shattering problem for a guy to have, maybe, but still. It was the kind of thing a dad taught his son. To make matters worse, Logan hadn't even realized he didn't know how until he'd stood in the high school bathroom, staring in a mirror with two uncooperative flaps of silk material in his hands, feeling embarrassed and helpless.

He felt the exact same way now. Helpless—and a little ashamed not to know facts that every other guy seemed to know automatically. How was he going to figure all this out?

"Sheriff?" He looked up to see the nurse, Melissa, smiling from the doorway. "There's somebody back here who'd like to meet you."

He jumped to his feet. "Is everything okay? How's Charlotte? Is the baby all right?"

"Everybody's fine."

"Are you sure?" The relief had his knees turning to jelly for the second time, but Melissa only laughed. Until today, he hadn't realized how heartless nurses could be.

"Why don't you come see for yourself? No," she said quickly when the rest of the family also stood. "Just him." She grinned at the collective groan. "Be patient. The rest of you will get your turn, but we need to give the little family some time alone first."

He heard disappointed sighs behind him as he strode out of the room, followed by Maggie's bright suggestion, "Melissa? Have a cookie!"

He nudged open the door to Charlotte's room and stopped short.

It felt different now. Before, the lights had been brighter, there'd been a sense of urgency and nerves as everybody bustled around preparing for the birth.

Now, the lights were soothingly dim and it all seemed more peaceful. Charlotte was propped up in the bed, covered with a pink blanket. She and Ruby were both absorbed in the tiny baby cuddled in her arms. He gave the baby a quick glance, but he couldn't see much except for a round little head covered with dark curls. So he looked back at Charlotte, trying to see for himself if she was truly all right.

She seemed to be. In fact, in the soft glow of the gentle lighting, she looked a lot more than all right.

Her hair was tangled and still damp. There was an IV taped to her arm, and her ill-fitting hospital gown was slipping off one shoulder. But as she gazed down at the bundle in her arms, the love shining in her face took his breath away.

He'd seen plenty of ugliness in his life—a good bit more than most people. There wasn't much of an upside to that, except that when he saw something beautiful, he had enough hard-won perspective to really appreciate it.

Right now, holding the baby she'd battled so hard to bring into the world, the baby she'd have to fight to keep, Charlotte was the most beautiful thing he'd ever seen in his life.

He pushed the door open wider, and Ruby glanced up.

She patted Charlotte's arm and whispered something Logan couldn't hear. Then she walked toward the door.

"Go on in, son," she said. "Meet your little boy."

He walked in, stopping awkwardly halfway to the bed. Charlotte looked up, and the familiar sweetness of her smile drew him the rest of the way.

"Isn't he gorgeous?" she whispered, tucking back the blanket so that Logan could get a better look.

Logan had been prepared to sidestep this question. He liked babies. He liked them a lot. But, in his private opinion, sunsets were gorgeous. So were dogwood trees in bloom, the ocean at dawn and, of course, Charlotte herself.

Newborn babies, on the other hand, looked like Winston Churchill.

He'd privately asked Ruby about this. *I can't lie*, he'd pointed out desperately. He'd gotten little sympathy from his practical mom.

You can't tell a brand-new mama that her baby's ugly, either, Ruby had responded tartly. *Never mind. Just say he's sweet. All babies are sweet, so that's no lie*.

But as it turned out, he could've skipped the worrying. Because this baby, Charlotte's baby, actually was kind of gorgeous.

He had a button nose and a mouth with a good shape to it, and an endearingly dopey way of opening his eyes halfway, rolling them around and then shutting them again. He also wasn't bald, which helped with the whole Churchill thing.

"Yeah," Logan agreed softly. "He is."

"Do you want to hold him?"

He did want to, desperately. And he equally desperately didn't. But he reached down and picked up the soft, warm bundle of brand-new human being, lifting him up, careful to steady his head.

As he did the baby's eyes peeped open, and Logan fell head over heels in love. It was as simple—and as complicated as that.

"Hi there," he murmured. He looked down at Charlotte. "Does he have a name?"

She nodded. "I'd like to call him Daniel. It's a strong name, I think."

"I like it." Logan looked back at the baby in his arms and smiled. "Hiya, Daniel."

Charlotte cleared her throat. "I'd like his whole name to be Daniel Tremaine Carter."

Logan froze. He looked down at her. "Carter?"

"Yes. I mean, if you're okay with that."

Okay with that. He started to answer, then found that he couldn't quite manage it.

"I've been thinking," Charlotte said. "His first name, Daniel, will be all his own. And the Tremaine part...well. I had to do some praying about that, honestly. But being a Tremaine is part of who he is, and I want to acknowledge it. There were so many things I loved about Dylan... at first. Those are the qualities I hope to see in Daniel, you know? The best part of who Dylan was, and who he could have been."

"I understand that." He swallowed. "That's a good thing, Charlotte. It's the right thing."

"But I'd like him to have your last name. You're the one I want to be his role model. I want him to look to you to learn how to be a good man." She paused. "We've talked about this, already—what your relationship is going to be, what a commitment it is. But it's different when it's just an idea." She nodded to the baby in his arms. "It doesn't get much more real than this. I need to know if you're still all in, if you still want to be Daniel's dad." She waited a second. "Do you?"

He looked down at the baby in his arms. His son.

"I've got to sit down."

She looked alarmed. "Maybe you should give me the baby."

"No, it's all right." Logan dragged over the chair and lowered himself into it carefully, holding Daniel against his chest. "It's okay. I've got him."

He dragged his eyes away from the baby and met her worried gaze straight on. "I've got him, Charlotte," he repeated.

He was making her a promise. Her mouth trembled, and he saw the tears coming into her eyes.

"Good," she whispered. "That's good."

"Excuse me?" Melissa poked her head through the door. "If I don't let the rest of your family in here, they're going to break down the door. You guys up for some quick visits?"

Logan glanced at Charlotte. "You don't have to—" he started, but she shook her head.

"No," she said. "It's fine. Bring them on in, Melissa. Daniel might as well meet the rest of his family."

Logan smiled, but he couldn't help noticing the way Charlotte worded it. Logan's family was Daniel's, maybe. But not hers.

Something about that twisted at his heart, but he didn't have much time to think about it before his siblings poured through the door in an excited rush, exclaiming over the baby.

It was two hours before they got rid of them all, and even then it took both Logan and Melissa to herd them out of Charlotte's hospital room. When he and Charlotte were finally alone again, they looked at each other.

"Whew," she said softly.

"Sorry. They can be a little overwhelming."

"Don't apologize. They're very sweet, especially… you know…considering the circumstances." She looked around her room. Every available space was crammed full of bears, balloons and flowers. She shook her head. "Generous, too. Do you think there's anything left in the gift shop?"

"Doesn't look like it." His happy mood had dimmed

at that *considering the circumstances* part. Why did she keep bringing that up?

"Logan?" He glanced over to find Charlotte frowning at him. "Are you okay?"

He forced a smile. "I'm supposed to be asking you that."

"I'm fine," she said firmly. "Just tired. In fact, since they're going to keep the baby in the nursery until the pediatrician checks him over, I think I might take a nap."

"That's a good idea."

"I know you got called away from work." She looked at the clock. "It's nearly six, so visiting hours will be over soon. Why don't you go check in with the sheriff's office and then go home and crash? You can come back tomorrow morning."

"You mean…leave you for the whole night?" He frowned. He knew husbands were allowed to stay if they wanted, and he'd already tested the reclining chair by her bed. He'd been prepared to keep vigil until the morning.

But Charlotte was nodding. "Sure. There's nothing you can do here, and I've already kept you from your work for the whole day."

"That doesn't matter." He didn't want to go. He wanted to stay right here, dividing his time between this room and the nursery, keeping a watchful eye on the two people topmost on his priority list right now.

He felt awkward saying so in the face of Charlotte's sensible suggestion. And the truth was, he probably should check in with the office.

But, still.

"Are you sure?"

"Daniel and I will be fine here. And you won't be far away, if I need you."

"Okay." He walked to the door, feeling like he'd left his heart behind. He turned to look back.

She waved at him from the bed, and his mind flicked to the last time he'd seen her in a hospital room.

This was different.

This room wasn't so sleek. Maybe it was even a little shabby. But balloons bobbed overhead, bright flower arrangements crowded along her windowsill, and Maggie had left the box of cookies handily within reach. This was the room of a woman people cared about.

Yes, he could leave Charlotte here. For a little while, anyway.

"I'll be back," he said. "First thing in the morning."

Her smile widened. "I know you will."

He detoured by the nursery, but the blinds were drawn. He considered knocking on the door to double-check on Daniel, but decided against it. He had a feeling he and his family had already stretched the nurses' patience to its limits.

He waited until he made it to the parking lot before turning on his radio. "101, 10-8," he said, notifying the evening dispatch that he was temporarily back in service.

The evening dispatcher rattled off a series of numbers with an alarming swiftness. "101, 10-19 to the SO."

Return to the sheriff's office. Logan frowned. The request itself wasn't that unusual, but there was a strange note in the dispatcher's voice that made the short hairs on the back of his neck prickle.

Something seemed off.

He clicked the button on the radio. "10-4."

The response clicked back. "10-18."

Logan frowned. That meant *fast.*

Yeah, something was wrong. He slid into the patrol car and hit the lights.

Chapter Twelve

When the phone beside Charlotte's hospital bed buzzed at seven the next morning, she knew who it would be before she picked it up.

"Did I wake you?"

She smiled at the concern in Logan's voice. "Hospitals aren't the best place for sleeping in. I've been awake for an hour. I've even had a shower." And felt a thousand percent better for it, too.

"So you're feeling okay? And Daniel's all right?"

"I'm fine." Charlotte glanced at the infant sleeping peacefully in the clear bassinette beside her bed. "Daniel is, too. All the nurses say he's doing wonderful, especially since he was a little early. No problems at all." She couldn't resist adding, "But you already know that. The nurse told me you'd called the desk three times already, checking on us."

She heard a soft, embarrassed chuckle. "Tattletales. Listen, Charlotte, I've got to take care of a few things in town, but then I'll come to the hospital. There's something I need to talk to you about."

"Is something wrong?"

"Nothing you need to worry about. I'll be there before long, okay?"

Charlotte frowned as she hung up the phone. Whatever Logan wanted to discuss, he didn't sound too happy about it.

A tiny fear uncoiled itself in her stomach. Was he having second thoughts? It was a lot to ask of any guy...a "for show" marriage and instant fatherhood.

Not that Logan Carter was just any guy, but still. She'd been surprised before, hadn't she? When Dylan had slid into his personal darkness so shortly after their marriage, it had blindsided her.

There was a knock on the door, and the morning nurse peeked in. "Hi! Listen, visiting hours haven't started yet, but you have an early bird out here. I don't see any harm in bending the rules. Are you up for company?"

"Sure." Maggie had told her she'd try to slip in for a quick visit before she opened the bakery. She'd outlined a plan to bribe her way past the desk by bringing along some fudge, which she'd described as "nurse catnip."

"I hope you saved me a piece," Charlotte started when the door opened. Then she stopped short.

Instead of Maggie, a middle-aged man walked into the room, smiling hopefully. "Charlotte?"

"Yes." She'd never seen him before, but there was something oddly familiar about him. She couldn't put her finger on it.

"It's good to meet you. Sorry to barge in like this, but I probably won't be in town too long. I didn't want to miss my chance to say hello to Logan's new wife." He walked up beside the bed. "I'm Marty."

He must be another one of Logan's many fans. She smiled.

"Hi, Marty." She accepted his offered hand, which

closed around hers with a warm friendliness. He certainly seemed to think she should know who he was, but she had no clue—except for that niggling feeling of familiarity. "Thanks for coming by."

"Oh, I wouldn't have missed this for the world! This the little fellow?" He beamed over the bassinette. "Well, now, isn't he a cute one?"

"Thank you." Charlotte studied him, still trying to figure him out. Shabby outfit, well-worn shoes. Not a man of means, then. "We think so."

"Hard to think of Logan being married, let alone being a daddy." The man shook his head. "Time sure flies, doesn't it?"

"It does."

The man had a charming smile, and he seemed harmless. Still, there was something about this fellow that didn't quite add up. Maybe it was the weak flabbiness of his jaw, or the slight shiftiness to his eye, but somehow he didn't seem like the sort of man Logan would be particularly friendly with.

An idea occurred to her. Maybe this was some kind of…professional acquaintance of Logan's. That could go in two very different directions.

"Marty, did you say you were just in town for a short while?"

"That's right." He reached down to tickle Daniel under his chin.

"Does Logan know you're here?"

"I didn't call ahead, if that's what you mean. But I expect I've made it onto his radar by now." The man glanced up and offered her an easy grin. "That's why I figured I'd best come along quick to see you. Unless I miss my guess, he'll be running me out of town shortly."

"Oh?" She felt around the bed rail for the nurse call

button and rested her finger on it. "Why would Logan run you out of town?"

He waved a hand gently. "No need for us to get into all that. It's a long story, and it would just spoil our nice visit. I came by because I wanted to have a word with you."

"About what?"

"This quickie marriage of yours hasn't gone over well in certain circles." He tilted his head and smiled sadly. "It's a real shame when a family goes to causing trouble for newlyweds, isn't it? And your mother-in-law in particular, well…" He shook his head. "She sure seems determined to kick up a fuss."

"Elizabeth sent you?"

"Well, not personally. A real nice private detective looked me up. Offered me a handsome sum to come over here and pay my respects. Make my presence felt in town, so to speak. Even paid for a fancy rental car."

"Why?"

"Like I told you. To cause trouble."

Charlotte pressed the nurse call button then reached over to gather Daniel into her arms. The baby protested, but she cuddled him protectively against herself. "You need to leave."

"No, no!" Marty held his hands up, looking alarmed. "I didn't mean to scare you. I was just explaining. Figured any wife of Logan's was sure to have a good appreciation for the truth—and you might be more inclined to hear me out than he would be. You can ask anybody. I wouldn't hurt a fly."

"Yes?" The nurse's voice came briskly over the intercom.

"Send security to my room," Charlotte said. "Now."

"On the way!" There was a clatter, and a code went out over the loudspeaker in the hall, accompanied by Charlotte's room number.

Marty backed away, looking appalled. "I never meant to upset you, Charlotte. If you want me to go, of course, I'll go. No need for any fuss. Honestly, that's not why I came. I only wanted to—"

Before he could finish the sentence, the door flew open. Logan strode inside.

"Charlotte, I heard the code when I came in the door. What's going on?" He stopped short and faced down her visitor, his eyes narrowed.

The two of them stared at each other for a long heartbeat before Marty broke the silence.

"Son, I'm afraid there's been a little misunderstanding."

Son? Charlotte's eyes darted between the two of them. Yes, there it was. That was why this man had looked so strangely familiar. He had Logan's straight nose, and there was something similar about the eyes.

Maybe Logan hadn't ever told her much about his dad, but in another way his silence had told her everything she needed to know.

"Your father was just leaving," she said.

"Everything okay here?"

Logan nodded at the security guard. "I've got this, Will. Thanks." He turned back to his father. "I'll walk you out."

"This isn't what you think."

"It never is." He pointed to the hallway. "Walk faster."

"I was only trying to help. I didn't mean to spook her. I figured I'd have a better chance talking to her than to you—"

"No chance." Logan cut him off firmly. He stopped at the elevator and stabbed the lobby button. "You have exactly zero chance of talking to her. Ever. Have I made myself clear?" As they stepped inside, an idea occurred to him. "Did you ask her for money? Because if you did—"

"No! No, I didn't. Not that I couldn't use a few dollars—" His father glanced up into Logan's face and quickly changed tactics. "But no. If you'd just listen to me for a minute. I was actually trying to help you."

"Really? Is that why you showed up here? You got the whole town stirred up. They called me to the office yesterday evening. They'd had reports of some man walking around town, introducing himself as my father."

"I am your father."

"Since the guy was asking a lot of questions and seemed not to know much about me, they figured it was some kind of scam." Even though he knew it wouldn't do any good, Logan jabbed the lighted elevator button again. "What kind of scam is it?"

"No scam." When Logan threw him a skeptical look, his father hurried to add. "Not this time. I had to ask questions. It's not like I knew where to find you. I didn't even know you were the sheriff until that private investigator told me." Marty shook his head. "I had to laugh. I mean, I've had more than one…unfortunate brush with the law, and here's my only son, a county sheriff. Who'd have seen that coming?"

Nobody who knew you. Logan didn't say the words aloud, but he was tempted to.

"I wanted to talk to you. It's like I was telling your girl back there, you two have some trouble coming."

"From you?"

"Take the daggers out of your eyes. No, not from me. Although that wasn't for lack of trying. That Tremaine woman down in Savannah, she's sure got it in for you."

Logan listened as his father reported being tracked down in Vegas by a private detective and asked to come to Cedar Ridge and identify himself as Logan's father. And if, it was implied, Marty should dabble in some criminal activities while visiting Roane County, preferably something worthy of the newspaper, he was assured that an interested party would happily make his bail.

Logan frowned.

"You agreed to this?"

His father got an all-too-familiar cagey look. "Agreed is a strong word."

The elevator doors opened on the ground floor. "You're here, aren't you?"

His father trailed him through the lobby and out into the parking lot. "Well, they were offering me a lot of money. Called it a charitable donation, but it was a payoff, all right. I was scraping the bottom of the barrel, son, and I don't mind telling you, it was a temptation."

And Martin Carter had never been good at resisting temptation. "Where are you parked?"

"Over here." Martin led the way to a nicer-than-average rental sedan. Logan raised his eyebrows and whistled.

"Exactly how much did they give you to come here and stir up stink, Dad?"

"More than you'd think it would be worth." Martin pulled keys out of the pockets of his baggy pants and weighed them in his hand. "They gave me enough money up front to set myself up in an apartment because they wanted me to stick around awhile. Offered to pay my living expenses. Said some fellow running against you in the next election wanted to talk to me."

Logan clenched his jaw. "That so?" He could well imagine what political capital Barton Myers could make of his aging grifter of a father. He also knew what kind of trouble this silver-tongued and sticky-fingered man would be likely to get into if he hung around Cedar Ridge for longer than a couple of hours. "You're not staying."

His father sighed. "I figured you'd say that. You sure?

I mean, I don't have to follow through with anything they want me to do, but it's a sweet deal. Might be sweet for both of us. We could even split the money, if you wanted. I mean, not even. But I'd give you a cut, if you'd be willing to let me stick around."

Logan blew out a long breath. That, he suspected, or something like it, was exactly what Findlay and Mrs. Tremaine hoped he'd do. "Safe travels, Dad."

His father looked disappointed. "Figured you'd say that, too. Well, give me some credit at least. I didn't have to tell you about it, now, did I? I could have just done what they wanted and took the money. Which, like I said, I had plenty of use for."

Logan frowned. "No, I guess you didn't have to tell me." Which raised a question. "Why did you?"

"Well, now, you're my son, no matter what water's gone under the bridge between us. I didn't like some rich woman trying to bring you down." The older man hesitated. "This Tremaine lady. How much do you know about her? She sure seems to have it out for you."

"It's not really about me. I'm just in the crossfire." He took the key ring from his father's hand, pressed the button and unlocked the car.

"Not a good place to be, not with people like that."

"I'm not worried."

"Maybe you should be." He shot Logan an uncertain look. "I know you don't have much respect for my opinion, and I can't say I blame you. But this is one time you might better listen to your old man. You drift off the straight and narrow often enough, you get a real good sense about folks. People like the woman you're dealing with are the most dangerous kind. They think they deserve to get what they want, and they don't much care what they have to do to get it. They'll roll you under the bus, then go order themselves a piece of pie and never think twice about it."

"You going to help her do that?"

"No, I'm not." His father straightened his shoulders. "But that only means she'll find someone else who will. Won't be too hard. Law officer like you, you've made some not-so-nice folks mad, I'm guessing. Could be one of them won't be too shy about stretching the truth about you, not for somebody with such deep pockets."

That was true enough. As fair as Logan tried to be, there were always some people who resented being made to behave themselves.

When he didn't answer right away, his father opened the car door and slid inside. "I guess I'd better be on my way. That's a real sweet family you got in there. I wish you the best with them." His father stared ahead through the windshield for a minute, working his mouth. "I know you'll be a real good father. Better than I was."

Real good? Logan wasn't so sure about that. But being better than Marty was a low bar to clear.

Still, something dawned on him. By telling him about Elizabeth's scheme, his father had done something nice... at a significant cost to himself. That was a first.

On impulse, Logan stuck out his hand. "I appreciate the heads-up."

Marty's eyes went wide as he accepted the courtesy, and his expression brightened. "You're welcome. I was glad to be able to help you out for once. The way I see it, family ought to help family with things like this. And other things like...you know...gas money."

Logan considered the sly hope in his father's eyes. Then he sighed and dug in his back pocket for his wallet.

Some things changed. Some things didn't.

Chapter Thirteen

"Come in and sit down." The following afternoon, Logan ushered Charlotte into the cabin as if she were made of spun glass.

He had Daniel's infant car seat slung over his free arm. The baby was dozing, and Logan set him carefully on the plank floor before helping Charlotte to a well-cushioned chair. Then he repositioned Daniel close beside her.

"Want something to drink? Or a snack? Maggie stocked the refrigerator."

"I'm fine," she assured him for the hundredth time. "You're the one who should sit down and put your feet up. You've been going around the clock for two days."

"I didn't just have a baby. I still can't believe the hospital lets new mothers go home this fast. Wait there." He disappeared outside, and she heard him taking the porch steps two at a time.

He didn't seem the worse for wear, but she doubted he'd slept much. Between keeping things running at the office—which didn't appear capable of functioning without him—and looking after her and Daniel, he'd been busy. He'd had plenty of help, though. Ruby and his siblings had all pitched in.

Her release from the hospital today had provoked another flurry of activity. Logan's family had stripped Charlotte's room of its flowers and gifts, then hauled them out to the cabin. Now they were tucked into every nook and corner, and earlier Logan had mentioned something about them getting Daniel's crib set up, too.

They'd tactfully vanished before Charlotte, Logan and Daniel arrived, leaving them to settle in. She had a hunch Logan had insisted on that.

"This is the last of them." He carried in another armload of gifts. These were from his coworkers at the sheriff's department. When they'd stopped there briefly on the way home, the entire department had crowded around Logan's truck. They'd exclaimed over the baby, safely settled with Charlotte in the back of the king cab, while cramming gifts into every available space in the vehicle.

It was a little overwhelming. People had even come running from the courthouse across the street, anxious for a glimpse of Daniel.

The whole town liked Logan, and everybody was curious about his new bride and the baby. Charlotte had fielded a few personal questions while his attention was distracted, but as soon as he'd figured out what was going on, he'd brought their impromptu visit to a quick end.

He'd apologized afterward for his friends' nosiness, but Charlotte hadn't minded. It was obvious how much these people cared about him. She'd seen not only respect, but also genuine affection in their eyes. Naturally they were concerned about their beloved sheriff's out-of-the-blue marriage.

The truth was, she had some new concerns herself, especially after his father's visit yesterday.

She'd tried to talk to Logan about it a couple of times, but he'd sidestepped her questions. That hadn't been particularly hard—they'd had a steady stream of visitors and little time for private conversations.

Now, though, they were finally alone, and it was high time that they talked this over.

"Logan, could you sit down, please? I want to ask you something."

His expression shifted into wariness. He must already suspect what she wanted to talk about. But all he said was, "Sure."

She waited until he'd settled on the couch, angling the baby carrier so he could see Daniel's face. "What did your father say about Elizabeth and her lawyer? What were they trying to do, sending him here?"

Logan sighed. "Charlotte—"

"I'd like to know, Logan." When he hesitated, she added, "Please."

She knew by the expression on his face that he didn't want to tell her. But he did, even though she had to prod him with a few questions to get the whole of it—or what she hoped was the whole of it.

She sat back in the chair, appalled. "I can't believe she did that. No," she amended sadly. "Actually, I can believe it. It's exactly the sort of thing she would do. I'm so sorry, Logan."

"Don't apologize. It's her fault, not yours. And it didn't work, anyway. Surprisingly enough, my father decided to be a stand-up guy. For once," he added, a resigned bitterness in his voice.

"I thought your dad was kind of sweet," she offered. "And he seemed harmless enough."

"He can slop sugar with the best of them when it suits him. Explains why he's been married more times than I can count. Women love him—to start with, anyway. Harmless might be a stretch, although in fairness the only harm he usually does is to people's bank accounts."

"Well, that's better than Elizabeth." She shook her head. "He's right, you know. She won't give up. Since this didn't work, she'll try something else."

"So what if she does?" Logan shrugged. "She may be rich, but at the core of it, she's just another bully, Charlotte. The best way to deal with bullies is to stand up to them." He smiled. "Trust me—I've been looking after myself for a long time. I grew up with an absentee mom and a two-bit grifter for a father, remember? Dad was good at conning people out of their money. Not so good at getting away with it. He always overplayed his hand, stayed just a little too long in the game. Dishonest people are like that. If you give them enough rope, they'll tie themselves in a knot every time. Mrs. Tremaine and that lawyer of hers will, too. You'll see." He stood and held out a hand. "Now if you're really feeling all right, I'd like to show you something."

He was changing the subject. She knew that, but she accepted his hand and let him help her to her feet.

"What is it?"

"Come and see."

He led her to the doorway of the cabin's larger bedroom, the one he'd insisted be hers when she'd moved in. He opened the door, and she sucked in a startled breath.

Logan and his sisters had been busy.

Last time she'd seen this space, it had been a simple, no-frills sleeping area, comfortable enough but with a decidedly masculine feel. Now it was a combination adult bedroom and nursery, decorated with a whimsical forest motif. The bed was covered with a thick leaf-sprinkled comforter, its headboard padded with a litter of pillows. A crib was nearby, sporting sheets printed with foxes, squirrels and pine trees. A comfortable rocker was positioned next to a changing table, stocked with baby essentials in wicker baskets. Daniel's name was spelled out over the crib, each letter in an individual frame, suspended against the log wall with a thick ribbon.

"Oh!" That one syllable was all she could manage.

"Do you like it?" Logan was watching her closely, gauging her reaction. "Maggie, Torey and Jina picked everything out. The only thing I was allowed to contribute was my debit card. They worked around the clock because they wanted it all fixed up when you came home from the hospital. Anything you don't like, we can change. I made sure they saved all the receipts."

His sisters had gone to so much trouble. She shook her head, struggling to speak around the lump in her throat. "I don't want you to change a thing. It's perfect." It was, too. Absolutely perfect, and a world away from the fussy nursery designs Elizabeth Tremaine's decorator had provided. "It's too much, though. I can't believe your family did all this."

"Not just my family. They're your and Daniel's family, too, now."

Her family, too. That just about did her in. Of course, it wasn't true, not really. She shook her head. "Well, but—"

"No buts." He tipped up her chin and looked into her eyes. "Families come together in a lot of different ways, Charlotte. My brothers and sisters and I know that better than most. Maybe we're not so typical, you and me and Daniel, but that doesn't mean we're not a family." He was smiling at her, and she didn't seem to be able to look away from him. "The truth is, you've been a part of my family since the day you plopped yourself down and announced that we were going to be friends. Remember?"

"I remember." She'd felt sorry for him. He'd had a

closed-down expression on his face, and he'd been sitting all by himself. So she'd decided to do the sad new guy a favor.

The irony of that brought her up short.

She'd thought she was doing *him* a favor.

And now...she looked around the sweetly decorated nursery, then up into the kind, strong face of this man who'd taken her considerable troubles onto his own shoulders without hesitation. The lump in her throat swelled, threatening to turn into tears.

"Charlotte?" A line formed between his brows, just north of his straight nose. "Is something wrong?"

She put her hands on either side of his lean cheeks and pressed in. "You," she said in a whisper, "are the best man in the whole world, Logan. Thank you. I don't know—" She couldn't go any further. Since words had failed her, she tiptoed to kiss him on the cheek.

At least, that's what she'd intended to do. But at the last minute, for some reason she was never sure of later, she changed course and kissed him on the lips instead. As his mouth molded to fit hers, she felt his astonishment mingle with her own.

It was all over in a second or two. Their kiss was short and innocent, and it shouldn't have meant anything in particular.

It shouldn't have, but it did. When she looked into his eyes, she knew he understood that as well as she did.

"Charlotte—"

"I'd better check on Daniel," she whispered, pulling away.

Daniel wasn't making a peep of noise, but Logan didn't argue. He nodded and stepped back. "You'd probably like to get him settled into his new crib, and you need to get some rest yourself. I have paperwork I need to work on. I'll boot up my laptop in my room so I don't disturb you."

"Okay."

He smiled then disappeared into his bedroom, before shutting the door behind him.

She thought it over as she went to collect Daniel, who was still napping peacefully in his infant seat.

Maybe Logan did have work to do. That was certainly possible. He seemed to have a lot on his plate, although he managed it without complaint. But she didn't think his quick retreat was really about backed up paperwork.

He was giving her space, respecting the agreement they'd made between them. One that hadn't included an impulsive kiss.

He didn't reappear until supper time, when he took command of the kitchen and warmed up a casserole Ruby had sent over. He seemed relieved at her suggestion that Ruby join them—and Ruby was ecstatic at the opportunity to do some baby snuggling.

Over the next few days they worked out a gentle routine. Ruby came over to the cabin, after Logan left for work, bringing the quilt. They sewed quietly together, looked after Daniel and Ruby took charge of supper most nights.

It was peaceful, and it was sweet, and between Logan, Ruby and Maggie—who also never missed a chance to drop by—Charlotte had all the help a new mother could have wished for.

The trouble was, now she'd started wishing for something else, too.

That silly, spur-of-the-moment kiss had awoken a part of her heart that had been sleeping for a long time. If anybody had asked her before, she'd have said easily that she loved Logan Carter. She'd have meant it, too.

But now, the feelings she had for him had shifted into

a new direction. She wanted to blame it on new motherhood, on the hormones and emotions that bobbed as erratically as the helium balloons they'd brought home from the hospital. In time, she assured herself, her feelings would go back to normal.

She told herself that. Repeatedly. The trouble was, by now she'd been around Logan long enough to recognize a lie—even when she was telling it to herself.

She didn't know what to do, or if she should do anything at all. She'd waited for Logan to comment on the kiss, but he hadn't. If anything, he was being even more careful to keep everything between them strictly friendly.

Maybe that should be her answer. But the longer she spent in close quarters with Logan, the happier she was—and the more unsettled she felt. It would have been easier if he hadn't been quite so…perfect.

A week after the birth, she put Daniel down for his morning nap, and picked up a pad to jot down some questions she wanted to ask the pediatrician at the infant's upcoming appointment. A list scribbled in Logan's firm handwriting caught her eye. *Yellow apples, chocolates, books.*

She smiled, and the secret feelings hiding in her heart stirred. There he went…being perfect again. Yellow apples were her favorites, and he'd brought her four beautiful ones yesterday when he'd come home from work. He'd gotten chocolates, too, hand-dipped ones Maggie had created and was trying out at the bakery. She'd assumed those things had been impulse purchases, but apparently not. Logan, as usual, had gone out of his way to bring her some sunshine.

It didn't help her confusion any that he was always doing things like that. Little, thoughtful things. Things that tempted her to believe that maybe his feelings, like hers, had crossed that very sensible line they'd set at the beginning.

She couldn't be sure, though, because Logan had always been a kind and generous guy—with everybody. She'd understood that at the hospital, when people had crowded into her room just because he was there. He made a habit of looking after people, like Ruby had told her. The fact that he was treating her so well didn't necessarily mean anything…romantic. Maybe he was just being himself— and holding up the end of the bargain they'd made.

That thought prickled sharply. She tore the list off the pad and started to drop it into the trash can, when the last item on the list caught her eye. Books?

He hadn't given her any of those. Although, come to think of it, hadn't he carried some books past her yesterday? He'd taken them straight into the bedroom. She hadn't thought much of it at the time—she'd been pretty distracted by those marvelous chocolates—but now it seemed strange. He'd brought library books home before, mysteries, mostly, and he'd always offered her first choice.

Of course, she had almost no time to read right now, but still. It was out of character for him not to even offer to share. She glanced at his bedroom door. It was slightly ajar, and after a moment's hesitation, she walked over and peeked inside.

Sure enough, three library books were stacked on his bedside table. Curious, she pushed the door wider and leaned in to scan the titles.

She grinned. No wonder he hadn't offered to share.

The book on the top of the pile was *Fatherhood Step by Step*. The title on the one beneath it made her chuckle— *Baby Daddy: The Guy's Guide to Connecting with Your Newborn*.

But the third book in the stack made her frown and drew her all the way into the room.

She picked it up and read the title again. *Alternate Careers for Law Enforcement Officers.*

An angry dread settled in the pit of her stomach. He must have chosen this one just in case Elizabeth's plan worked and one of her schemes cost him the election. He hadn't hinted to her that he was concerned about that—but obviously he was.

He should be, knowing Elizabeth.

This wasn't good. Law enforcement meant more than a salary to Logan. It was a passion, a calling, the way her work with fabric had been in the beginning. Maybe he didn't say much about it, but it was easy to see how he felt about what he did. He always went above and beyond, giving his best to the people of Cedar Ridge day after day, quietly, faithfully. Keeping them safe, keeping danger and disorder away from them, as best he could.

Now he was putting the job he loved on the line. For her and for Daniel.

Charlotte stood there for a minute, her heart beating hard. Oh, she hated this, hated seeing a good man like Logan attacked just because he happened to be standing between Elizabeth Tremaine and something she wanted. Her own passion for art and to a large degree her marriage had been damaged by Elizabeth—and for the same reason. Because Elizabeth expected people to fall in line with her wishes. When they didn't do it voluntarily, she rolled up her designer sleeves and bullied them until they did.

Logan's advice echoed in her memory. *The best way to deal with bullies is to stand up to them.*

He was doing that now, for them. Knowing him, he'd keep doing it, no matter what it cost him.

And she was standing by and letting him.

Charlotte flinched. The unfairness of that chilled her.

When her life had fallen apart, Logan had gone to Savannah and yanked her to safety. He'd sheltered her and comforted her. Unbelievably, he'd even blasted through the walls of his comfort zone and married her.

At the time, she'd been exhausted, pregnant and emotionally bankrupt. She'd needed his help, and she'd deeply appreciated it. But enough was enough.

It was time she helped him, for a change.

Elizabeth and her selfish schemes had to be dealt with, but Logan shouldn't have to do it alone. And he certainly shouldn't lose his job over it.

This was Charlotte's fight, and it was high time she stepped in.

She strode out of his room and went straight for her phone. Before she could think better of it, she punched in an all-too-familiar number.

It was answered on the second ring.

"It's about time," her mother-in-law said.

The next morning, Logan walked out of his bedroom, straightening his badge and sniffing hopefully.

Sure enough, the aroma of fresh coffee was in the air.

He headed toward the kitchen. Charlotte was already there, dressed in yoga pants and a loose-fitting shirt.

"Good morning! I hope you have time for some breakfast."

He blinked. She'd sure gone all out. The table was neatly set, orange juice in small glasses—where had those come from? A sweet roll drizzled with white frosting rested on a plate at his spot at the table.

"Good morning." He generally made do with the stale doughnuts and coffee in the office breakroom. "I'll make the time, thanks. This looks great."

It did, and he could get used to waking up to this. Still, she was up and down with the baby during the night, and he didn't want her overdoing. He was perfectly capable of cooking for himself.

He bowed his head, said a silent grace and then decided he'd better set things straight.

"Look, I don't expect you to fix me breakfast."

"I didn't, not really." She tucked Daniel into a baby swing his sister had loaned them. "Maggie made the cinnamon rolls, and Ruby dropped them off yesterday. I just warmed them up and made coffee."

Well, in that case. His guilty feelings somewhat resolved, he picked up his fork and took a big bite.

"How'd Danny do last night?" he asked as soon as he could speak. Charlotte seemed a little stressed this morning. Maybe she was tired.

"*Daniel* did really well." They were having a good-natured feud about whether nicknames were allowed. "He only woke up once, and after I nursed him, he went right back to sleep."

"Atta boy." Logan reached over and touched the tiny boy's nose. He squirmed and stretched in his footie pajamas.

"Logan, could I ask you a favor?"

There it was again, that hint of nerves. Yeah, something was up. She didn't have to be nervous asking him for favors. Surely she'd figured that out by now.

"Of course." He tasted the coffee and smiled. "Spoiler alert, I'm probably going to say yes. Anybody who gives me coffee this good first thing in the morning can have anything I've got."

Her answering smile didn't quite make it to her eyes. "I was wondering—could I use your truck today? I'd like to take a trip into town."

Was that what this was about? "Sure you can. Anytime. You don't have to ask."

She looked relieved. "That's really nice of you."

He frowned. "We're married, Charlotte. Whatever I have is yours. Speaking of that." He dug into his pocket for his wallet. "Here."

She accepted the plastic rectangle with a puzzled look. "What's this?"

"I ordered you a debit card." Pulling a pen from his pocket, he scribbled four digits on his napkin and pushed it toward her. "That's the code."

"Oh, Logan." She held the card back out to him. "You didn't have to do that."

"The account belongs to you as much as it does me. Feel free to use the money for whatever you need—groceries, baby stuff, clothes, whatever." She looked unconvinced, so he pressed gently. "I'd feel better if you took it. I don't want you to be in a pinch and not have access to cash."

She bit her lip, then nodded. She didn't look happy, but she set the card beside her plate. "Thank you very much, Logan. What little money I had left in my account after settling Dylan's debts is nearly gone. I really appreciate this."

She sounded so formal. It irritated him a little. "You don't have to thank me. My money's yours, same as the truck. I mean that."

"I know you do." She reached across the table and took his hand. "And that's exactly why I do have to thank you."

Her fingers, slim and strong, curved around his. There was something about that, something about holding a woman's hand at breakfast while a baby kicked his feet in a swing decorated with forest animals…it did really funny things to a man's heartbeat.

"There's plenty of gas in the truck," he said. "And I had new tires put on it a month ago."

Why was he blabbering about tires? But she squeezed his hand and seemed to be blinking back tears.

"That's sweet of you to tell me. It's silly, but I'm feeling a little nervous driving Daniel into town by myself for the first time."

He frowned. "If it would make you feel better, I'll drive you in myself. I'll let the office know I'll be late. Or I could take a long lunch, and we could—"

"No." She refused so quickly that he was startled. "I don't want to take up your time. I know it's interfered with your work, helping us like you have."

"I don't mind." His instincts prickled again. Yeah, something was definitely off. She was jumpy, and she wouldn't look straight at him. If he hadn't known better, he'd think she wasn't being completely honest with him.

"Thanks, but I'd rather go by myself. There's a...personal errand I need to run."

"Oh. Okay." So that was it. He relaxed, relieved. He didn't know much about being married, but he knew when a woman said a subject was personal, a smart man backed away and minded his own business.

Since Danny's birth, Charlotte and Maggie had put their heads together more than once, talking quietly. When he'd cast a worried glance in their direction, his brother-in-law Neil had given him a sharp shake of the head.

Don't ask, Neil had warned. *Trust me.*

"I'll have to venture out by myself sooner or later," Charlotte was saying now. "I'll be fine."

He was tempted to ask all sorts of questions...where she was going...what she needed. How he could help. Instead, he took the last bite of his cinnamon roll and washed it down with another slug of coffee.

No hovering, he reminded himself.

"I'd better get to work, then. If you need anything, call

me." He stood and cleaned up after himself, setting his dishes in the sink.

"I will." Charlotte smiled at him with an artificial brightness as she rose from the table. "Thanks, Logan."

"You're welcome." He leaned over to look into Daniel's face. "Bye, Danny."

He heard Charlotte's sigh and chuckle behind him, and the clink of dishes as she cleared the rest of the table.

The baby squirmed, working on focusing his eyes. For a second, they seemed to catch on Logan's face.

"Hi, buddy," Logan said. The baby made a soft grunting sound and wiggled around again.

He really wasn't bad looking. Okay, maybe there was a slight Churchill resemblance, but Danny was way cuter than other babies. Logan fished his phone out.

"*More* pictures?" Charlotte asked. "Didn't you take about a dozen yesterday?"

"Gotta keep his fans happy. People at the office want to see new ones every day."

"Send them to me, too."

"Okay." He glanced at the time on his phone before he slipped it back into his pocket. He ought to already be on the road. Instead, he reached down and snapped open the little seatbelt, lifting the baby into his arms.

"You're going to be late." Charlotte pointed out behind him, an amused exasperation in her voice. At least she was sounding more like herself now.

"I don't care." He didn't. He gently positioned the baby against his chest, careful to find a spot between all the metal parts bristling on his uniform. The infant smelled clean and sweet, and his round head wobbled, brushing against Logan's cheek. His heart went into a ridiculous clench. "You're the best little guy," he murmured, patting the tiny back.

"Be careful," Charlotte warned. "He just ate, and—"

Before she could finish her sentence, the baby belched, spitting a mouthful of soured milk onto Logan's shirt.

"Oh, no!" She snatched a paper towel from the dispenser, dipped it in the dishwater and hurried over. She collected the baby and dabbed, one-handed, at the splotch on Logan's chest. "Your uniform!"

"It's all right."

"I couldn't get him to burp this morning," Charlotte fretted as she wiped. "I'm so sorry."

"My own fault for picking up a loaded baby," Logan said lightly. She was standing so close to him, dabbing at his chest. Her hair smelled like flowers, and the scent of it drew him back to when she'd surprised him with that kiss.

He'd been trying really hard not to think about that. But just now, he couldn't think of anything else—except maybe how much he'd like to take her into his arms and kiss her again, the baby snuggled sweetly between them.

"Logan?"

He blinked. She'd been talking to him, and now she looked puzzled.

"I asked if you needed to change your shirt? I got the yucky stuff off, I think, but it's still damp."

"What?" He glanced down at her and wished he hadn't. Standing so close, her face tilted up to his… He swallowed. "No, I'd better get to work."

"But—"

"Trust me—nobody's going to think twice about this." Except him, of course. He already knew he'd be thinking twice about a lot of things. "I'll see you later, Charlotte. Okay?"

"Okay." She still looked worried, but she nodded. "See you later."

The splotch had nearly dried by the time he arrived at

the department, but that didn't stop everybody who saw him from commenting on it. Before he made it back to his office, he'd been given baby-burping tips, spot-removing tips and a package of cloth diapers that would, he was assured, save the day if he'd put one over his shoulder before picking Danny up.

He tossed the diapers aside, turned on his computer and settled into his chair to check emails. But while the machine whirred to life, he found himself reaching for his phone and scrolling back to the newest pictures.

Yeah. The kid wasn't bad looking at all.

He was interrupted by a buzz from the department's inside line. "What is it, Marla?"

"Sheriff," the dispatcher whispered, "that man is here."

"What man?" Logan frowned. "Findlay?"

"No, not him. The other one. He's asking to see you."

The other one. He sighed. Great. So much for a happy morning. "Let him through."

A few seconds later, his father stood framed in the doorway. "Your secretary said I should come on back."

"She's not a secretary. She's a radio dispatcher. I thought you'd left town." *Hoped. Hoped you'd left town.* He didn't say that, but he didn't have to. His tone made it clear enough.

"I did. But I drove back in this morning. I…uh…felt like I needed to talk to you face-to-face."

Logan leaned back in his chair, instantly wary. He didn't like this. He didn't like the guilty look on his father's face, and he distrusted anything that his father wanted to talk about face-to-face. "About what? If you want more money—"

"No, no. It's not that. I just wanted you to hear it straight from me that I had nothing to do with it."

"Nothing to do with what?"

"You have to believe me. After we talked, I went straight out of town." His father was talking earnestly. "I didn't even stop the car until I was outside your city limits."

"City doesn't belong to me. The sheriff oversees the county." He tilted his head sideways.

"I didn't stop in the county either. And when that lawyer called, I didn't answer the phone. I listened to the voice mail, but I didn't know what he was talking about. It wasn't me. I want you to know that."

"What wasn't you?"

"Whoever got Charlotte to change her mind."

Logan bolted out of his chair. "Got Charlotte to change her mind about what?"

His father took a quick step backward, holding his hands up. "All I know is that the lawyer told me they'd be depositing money in my account because Charlotte had called the mother-in-law and agreed to a meet. He seemed to think I'd kept up my end of the bargain, but I didn't have a clue what he was talking about."

Logan's mind flashed to what Charlotte had said this morning about a personal errand—and to that nervousness he'd picked up on.

That had something to do with all this. He was sure of it.

He felt sick. He needed to know what was going on. Maybe she hadn't left the cabin yet. He'd drive back there and check.

"I've got to go," he said as he brushed past his father. "Thanks," he added awkwardly. "Marla? I'll be 10-6 for a while." He strode past her workstation on his way to the door.

Busy, unless it's an emergency. Marla looked up. "Something wrong?" she called after him.

He pretended he didn't hear her as he walked out the door. He'd never done that before.

Lately he'd been pretending about a lot of things. It looked like he hadn't been the only one. And it was time—past time—for that to stop.

Chapter Fourteen

Charlotte forced herself to stay on the bench at Cedar Ridge's puppy park as her mother-in-law walked along the sidewalk in her direction. It wasn't easy.

She could handle this, she reminded herself. She had to, for Logan's sake.

For both their sakes.

She took a deep breath, squared her shoulders and got to her feet.

Elizabeth looked annoyed. No surprise there. Dylan's mother wasn't accustomed to being told what to do—especially not by Charlotte.

The surprise had been her agreement to drive to Cedar Ridge, but it was easy to see why she had. The hunger in her expression when she glanced at Daniel made Charlotte's heartbeat quicken. She snuggled her son closer, and Elizabeth frowned.

"Was this really necessary?" She gestured at the pretty park, dotted with scampering dogs and their owners. "I drove for hours to come *here*? We couldn't have met somewhere closer to Savannah? Perhaps someplace indoors?"

"It's hard for me to travel very far these days." Besides, she'd thought it safer to meet here—on Logan's turf, and her own. In a public place, so hopefully things could stay civil.

Hopefully.

Elizabeth wasn't listening. Her attention was focused on Daniel. The older woman's professionally sculpted neck pulsed, and for the first time in Charlotte's memory, her mother-in-law didn't seem sure what to say.

"As you see, I came. Alone, as you asked. Am I finally going to be allowed to see my grandson now?" When Charlotte didn't answer, Elizabeth made an impatient noise. "Please?"

"Of course." When she angled her son's face toward his grandmother, Elizabeth's chilly composure slipped away, and she gasped.

"Oh! He looks exactly like Dylan! Give him to me," she commanded, holding out her arms. When Charlotte didn't comply, Elizabeth looked up from the baby's face. The two women regarded each other for a moment. Elizabeth set her jaw. "Forgive me," she said coldly. "That was ill-mannered. May I please hold him, Charlotte?"

"Why don't you sit down?" It was a testimony to how badly Elizabeth wanted to get her hands on the baby that she dropped onto the leaf-littered bench with no regard for her creamy linen slacks. Overriding her sense of reluctance, Charlotte settled Daniel into his grandmother's arms.

Elizabeth murmured as she traced the baby's face with one well-manicured hand. "Oh, you're lovely," she whispered. "So much like your father. You have his nose and his eyes. You'll be a handsome man, just like him. And you're going to have a beautiful life, the best possible life. Grandmother will see to that, don't you worry."

Charlotte settled beside her, watching closely. She'd never seen Elizabeth show this much emotion. Even when

Dylan had died, she'd been remote and icy cold. At the funeral, she'd stood beside the grave in her impeccable black dress, her face expressionless—except, of course, when she'd looked in Charlotte's direction.

"Elizabeth, I didn't only ask you here to see Daniel. I want to discuss this scheme you cooked up with Logan's father."

Elizabeth didn't glance away from the baby—or deny the accusation. "Desperate times call for desperate measures. Although I never thought I'd see the day when I'd make a bargain with a criminal." She flicked a look in Charlotte's direction. "You've married into a regrettable family."

Charlotte lifted her chin. "I have a habit of that."

Elizabeth's eyebrow twitched at the return jab. "Don't be ridiculous. We both know your marriage to this backwoods sheriff is a complete farce, designed to give you an advantage in the custody battle."

"Like you said. Desperate times call for desperate measures."

Elizabeth regarded her for a moment, a glimmer of surprise in the older woman's eyes. "Touché," she admitted lightly. "One thing does tend to lead to another, doesn't it? It was because Findlay assured me that my chances of gaining custody were…less than optimal that I hired a private investigator. Who, unlike your new father-in-law, didn't disappoint. He's produced quite a lot of juicy tidbits."

"He's lying to you, then. Logan hasn't done anything wrong."

"You're right. That sheriff of yours is annoyingly honest. However, that's not a family trait, it seems." Elizabeth lifted her eyebrows and tsked her tongue. "I can certainly sympathize. It's so difficult when someone disgraces the family name. I have some firsthand experience with that."

Thanks to you.

The unspoken accusation was clear. In the past, Charlotte would have let it go.

But things were different now.

"I didn't disgrace the Tremaine family, Elizabeth. Your son did."

"As usual, you're incorrect. Disgrace implies publicity. Dylan had his issues, but at least he—and we—had the sense to keep them quiet. All families have problems, but the correct thing is to deal with them privately. As I've explained to you before, when dirty laundry is exposed to the public, it can have unpleasant consequences." She paused. "To a small-town election, for example."

Charlotte frowned. "Is that a threat?"

"Take it as you will."

"You won't get custody of Daniel, even if Logan does lose the election." Charlotte's eyes narrowed as she watched Elizabeth's face. "You already know that. Then why would you do it?" She shook her head. "I don't know why I ask. Because you're spiteful."

"This has nothing to do with spite. It has to do with business, something you've never had much of a head for. I want a relationship with my grandson. No," she said, when Charlotte made a sharp noise, "I didn't say custody. I said a relationship."

Charlotte studied her. "Go on."

"I'm prepared to make you an offer."

This wasn't going the way she'd planned, but she wasn't entirely surprised. Trust Elizabeth Tremaine to treat being a grandmother like a business negotiation. She sighed. "What kind of offer?"

"A good one, one that will benefit this child socially and financially. Obviously, there are some caveats. You'll put an end to this sham of a marriage, and you'll move back to Savannah. Afterward, you'll be provided with a house of your own and enough capital to restart that little dress-making hobby of yours."

Charlotte's Originals. She hadn't thought about her business in weeks. "I doubt that's possible after the Sheridan wedding."

Elizabeth dismissed the objection with a wave of her hand. "The Sheridans are no match for the Tremaines. I'll settle Pippa and Daphne, and I have plenty of other friends who'd be delighted to have my daughter-in-law design a dress for them. If you'd prefer not to work, that can also be arranged. I'll set up an allowance. Of course, there'll be a trust fund for the baby, although his name will have to be legally changed first."

"I'm not changing his name."

"Of course you are. I must say, it was rather nasty of you, putting such a ridiculous name on his birth certificate. However, it can be remedied easily enough, and he'll carry the name that is his legacy. Dylan Carson Tremaine III."

"My son's name is Daniel Tremaine Carter."

Elizabeth blew out an impatient sigh. "You're being impossible."

"I'm being honest. It's something I learned from that backwoods sheriff you're so annoyed with. And if you want a relationship with your grandson, you'll have to start being honest, too. Especially about Dylan." She took a deep breath. "He was an alcoholic, Elizabeth, and an abusive husband."

"Charlotte, I will not sit here and—"

"Denying it doesn't change the truth. You know what he was like, Elizabeth. How he treated me. You *know*."

Elizabeth's mouth trembled. "My son had his struggles, but—"

"He had more than struggles. He had some very serious problems." Charlotte set her jaw and met her mother-in-law's eyes. "And what happened to him was tragic, but it wasn't my fault."

They stared at each other for a long moment while dogs' happy barks sounded in the background.

For the first time ever, Elizabeth looked away first. "I realize that. I shouldn't have blamed you. I was just… angry about you calling the police on him the night he died. And yes, I knew he was…mistreating you. It's why I encouraged the two of you to move into my house. You were pregnant, and I thought if I were close by, maybe he wouldn't…" The older woman cleared her throat. "Obviously, the idea wasn't a success."

Charlotte sat back on the bench. "I didn't know that was your intention."

Elizabeth smoothed Daniel's blanket. "I loved my son, Charlotte. I simply didn't know how to handle him." She swallowed. "I suppose under the circumstances I can't blame you for wanting revenge, but—"

"I'm not interested in revenge, but I won't be bullied anymore, either. If you want me to come back to Savannah, if you'd truly like to have a relationship with Daniel, then you're going to do it on my terms."

Elizabeth studied Charlotte then looked into Daniel's sleeping face for several long seconds. Finally, she nodded, one short, resigned nod.

"Name them." she said.

Fifteen steps.

Logan made it to the kitchen, turned on his heel and started back across the living room. It took exactly fifteen steps.

He knew because he'd counted. Several times. For the last hour it had taken every distraction he could invent to keep from jumping in his patrol car and radioing an all-points bulletin on his own truck.

That would be an overreaction. He knew it, but that didn't make the waiting any easier. He was worried out of his mind about Charlotte and Danny.

She hadn't told him. That's what his brain kept circling back to. She'd kept her plans a secret this morning, even though she'd already made the arrangements to meet Elizabeth Tremaine.

Why hadn't she told him?

He didn't know, but the deception, innocent as it might have been, had hit him hard. Charlotte had shut him out of something important, and it hurt.

A lot.

His own pain was the least of his problems. He had no idea where Charlotte was meeting Elizabeth, he didn't know why and he didn't know when she was planning to come back. He'd raced home, hoping to find her still here, or at least a note explaining things.

He'd been disappointed. No Charlotte, no Danny, no note. Nothing.

He'd reassured himself that was a good sign. She'd have told him if she was going far or planning to be away for long.

Then again, maybe not. He knew from personal—and professional—experience that once people started keeping secrets, things went downhill fast.

In fairness, she wasn't the only one keeping secrets. Since that kiss—and maybe even longer than that—he'd been sidestepping the truth about how he felt about Charlotte. He, Sheriff Logan Carter, the guy whose reputation hinged on his honesty, hadn't even been honest with himself.

To make matters worse, half an hour ago, he'd done something else he'd never imagined himself doing.

He'd searched Charlotte's bedroom.

Except for when he'd helped put together Danny's crib, he'd never gone into her room unless the door was open, and he knew he was welcome. He'd tried to be extra careful about respecting her privacy. Her relationship with Dylan had done a number on her trust where men were concerned.

But today, after only the briefest wrestling match with his conscience, he'd opened the door and barged in, then checked her closet to see if she'd taken her things.

As near as he could tell, all her clothes were there, and the small suitcase she'd carried to the hospital was still parked on its shelf. He'd felt relieved, until he'd remembered that Elizabeth Tremaine could buy an entire store full of clothes for her and doubtlessly would, if that meant she could entice Charlotte to bring Danny back to Savannah.

He hated the idea of Charlotte facing up to that she-dragon alone. If she was determined to meet with the woman, he should've been standing right beside her. He would have been, if she'd given him the choice.

But she hadn't, and that was killing him. So, he paced, and prayed and worried.

He hadn't felt like this since…he'd never felt like this. As if his heart was walking around outside his body, somewhere he couldn't protect it, leaving him with an aching emptiness in his chest.

Logan froze in midpace when he heard the truck pulling into the yard. Charlotte was back. He started for the door, then stopped and forced himself to wait.

She came inside, diaper bag looped over one arm, carrying Danny asleep in his carrier.

"This is a nice surprise." She shut the door then turned toward him. He watched her read his expression, watched her face change as she realized why he was home.

That he knew where she'd been.

"I was going to tell you," she said softly. "About meeting with Elizabeth. I was always going to tell you."

"After." He made the clarification equally quietly. "You were going to tell me after." He paused. "Because I'd want to come along, and you wanted to keep me out of it."

She drew in a long breath. "Yes."

She wasn't telling him anything he didn't already know, so it shouldn't have hurt like it did.

"I understand."

"No, you don't. Let me put Daniel in his crib, and I'll explain."

When he nodded, she headed for her room. Almost against his will, he followed as far as the doorway, watching as she settled her baby into the crib.

Her baby. Not his.

Hers.

Once Elizabeth was running the show again, he'd lose Danny, too.

The truth of that hit him hard, but without as much pain as he'd have expected. Not, he realized, because it didn't hurt, but because after a point, there was only so much agony he could register. He'd blown the top off that scale earlier today, when he'd realized that the choice Charlotte had made today was his fault.

He shoved the thought back. He'd deal with that later—he'd have to, and it wouldn't be fun. Right now, this wasn't about him.

She finished settling Danny—Daniel, he corrected himself silently—and glanced up, catching his eye.

Then she flinched and looked away.

It was a small thing. Probably nobody else would have picked up on it, but he noticed everything about Charlotte. And that little wince made it all click into place.

He knew what she was about to tell him.

He waited until she came back out, until the door was closed, leaving a crack so they could hear the baby if he cried. Waited until she'd settled on the sofa beside him, an empty cushion between them. He could tell she was having trouble figuring out how to say what she needed to say.

So, he said it for her.

"You worked something out with your mother-in-law." There was a brief pause. "Yes."

"And it means you and Daniel are going back to Savannah."

A longer pause this time. "Yes. At least for a while."

He wanted to ask for details about the arrangement she'd made, to double-check that she hadn't been taken advantage of, but he restrained himself. If she'd wanted his input, she'd have clued him in way before now.

She cleared her throat. "How'd you find out that I'd called Elizabeth?"

"Apparently Elizabeth thought my father had done what they'd asked, and that was why you set up the meeting. He was worried I'd blame him."

"You shouldn't. He wasn't the reason I called. At least," she amended, "he wasn't the main reason."

"I don't think it matters now." He drew in a breath. "Is this deal you've hashed out with Elizabeth something you can live with?"

"Yes." She sounded certain. That was good, he guessed. As good as things could be right now. "I'll stay in Savannah with Daniel long enough to get things straightened out. I left everything hanging there…my business, our belongings. Those things have to be dealt with. It's my mess, and it's not fair to expect Elizabeth to cope with it. And she'd like to spend some time with Daniel, of course."

So Dylan's mother had changed tactics, casting herself as a victim and a doting grandmother. Smart. It was the one approach Charlotte couldn't resist.

"So you two are back on good terms?"

Charlotte sighed. "That's a stretch, but I think we've reached an understanding."

He nodded. Waited. Then made himself say it. "I guess we'd better see about getting an annulment."

Her eyes widened. "Logan—"

"It makes sense. The marriage has served its purpose. Getting it dissolved shouldn't be hard to do. I'll tell Eric to get things rolling."

Her knuckles had gone white, but when she spoke her voice was calm. "You're upset about me meeting with Elizabeth without telling you. I'd like to explain about that, if you'll let me."

"You don't owe me any explanations."

"I owe you a lot more than that!" She spoke sharply. "An apology, for starters. I know how important honesty is to you. I wanted to handle this by myself, but I should've realized how upset you'd be about me going behind your back."

He caught her gaze with his and held it. Time for him to come clean. "If anybody should be apologizing, Charlotte, it's me. You're not the only one who's been keeping secrets. I have too, and I've been really…selfish."

That surprised her. For a second she didn't seem to know what to say. "I don't know about the secrets, but selfish? You can't be serious. Look what you've done for Daniel and me, how you've taken care of us. You take care of everybody—Ruby, your brothers and sisters. The whole town. You're the least selfish man I've ever met."

She obviously believed what she was saying, but he

knew better. He had to tell her, because he couldn't let a lie stand between them.

She mattered too much for that.

"There are lots of different ways to be selfish, Charlotte. Looking after people can be one of them, if you do it like I do sometimes." When she started to protest, he interrupted her. "You know it. On some level you do. All the times I bugged you, asking how you were feeling, pestering the life out of you." He rubbed a hand through his hair. "I do that with everybody. I mean well. I always do. That doesn't mean I get it right. I'm sorry I put you in a position where you felt you couldn't be honest with me."

"Don't you dare apologize to me!"

She'd spoken so angrily that he blinked. "What?"

"And stop calling yourself selfish." He'd never seen Charlotte so mad. "You married me, Logan, so I wouldn't lose custody of my baby. Selfish? That's the most *unselfish* thing I've ever heard of."

"It wasn't as unselfish as you think." Much as he wanted to, he couldn't let her keep making excuses for him. "Of course I wanted to help you, Charlotte. I still do. I always will. But there's another reason I jumped on Eric's suggestion about us being married. My only excuse for not being honest with you is that I didn't understand it myself."

She'd gone very still, her eyes fixed on his. "Didn't understand what, Logan?"

He squared his shoulders and braced himself.

"That I'm in love with you."

Charlotte stared at him, all her protests forgotten. "*What* did you just say?"

"Maggie and the rest of them were right all along. The real reason I wanted us to get married is because I've fallen in love with you." He rubbed at his face. "Told you I'd been keeping a secret. When my family finds out about this, they're going to be impossible to live with."

"You love me." She stared at him, her brain fumbling to catch up. "You mean like...*love* love me?"

"Yeah."

"Since...when?"

"I'm not sure." He furrowed his brow. "I've been trying to figure that out. A long time, I think. Maybe even right from the start. Maybe always."

"Always." She repeated the word. *Their w*ord. He winced.

"I never planned to lie to you."

That much she believed. The rest of it she wanted to believe. Oh, how she wanted to believe it, but it seemed so incredible.

It also didn't add up. "Let me get this straight. You're in love with me. And you want an annulment."

"I think it's the best thing given the circumstances." He threw her a rueful glance. "How's that for ironic?"

"It's not ironic. It's the dumbest thing I've ever heard."

He'd been studying his hands, but he glanced up at her tone. "I never meant to wreck our friendship."

She made an impatient noise. "You couldn't ever wreck our friendship. It's beyond that. It's like—" she gestured helplessly "—the ocean," she finished. "What we have is like the ocean. Storms blow, hurricanes, even, and things get choppy and messy on the surface, but the water goes too deep for that to really matter. We'll always be friends, Logan. Always."

There it was. Their word again.

He squared his shoulders. "I'm glad you feel that way. I still plan to be there for Danny, as much as I can, in whatever way you'd like me to. But where you and I are concerned..." He trailed off. "I have to be honest—"

"Of course, you do."

"I'm not sure I can just be friends with you anymore. Maybe someday that'll change. I hope so. But...not right now."

Her heart thudded hard. This, she knew, was one of those rare, dangerous moments when everything important hung in the balance. She didn't understand why they always seemed to come right out of the blue. She'd have preferred some advance notice because if she handled this wrong, the regret would echo in her life for years.

But Logan wasn't the only one who had to be honest. She sent up a silent, desperate prayer and looked him straight in the eye.

"I said we would always be friends," she repeated. "And I meant it. No matter what. But I never said we had to be *just* friends."

And she leaned across the cushion and kissed him.

Chapter Fifteen

It was hard to think when you were kissing Logan Carter. But in the back of Charlotte's pleasantly distracted mind, one fact sparkled with a dazzling brightness.

He loved her. He'd said so, and he never lied.

Not on purpose, anyway.

He broke the kiss and pulled back, an astonished wariness in his eyes.

"What are you doing?"

"Trying to tell you that I'm in love with you, too."

She waited to see the joy she was feeling dawn on his face. For a split second, it did. Then it dimmed.

"Charlotte—" he started. Then he shook his head. "Since when?"

"What?"

"You asked me that question, and I answered it. I'd like to hear your answer, too."

She frowned. "I don't know, exactly. Does it matter?"

"It might. Was it before or after you found out that your mother-in-law had hired my father to hurt my chances in the election?"

"Logan, what are you getting at?"

"We both know you've always been drawn to people

you feel sorry for." He shook his head. "Come to think of it, that's how we met."

"That has nothing to do with how I feel about you now. I could wonder the same thing, by the way. Given everything you've just told me, maybe the only reason you think you love me is because I needed your help."

"Needed. Past tense. And like I said, I think I've always been in love with you."

"How do you know I haven't always been in love with you, too?"

He looked her straight in the eye. "Because you married somebody else, Charlotte. Some other guy you felt sorry for, if I'm remembering right."

Okay, that hurt. Her heart twisted. "That was a mistake. Now I'm married to you, and I don't want an annulment."

"Neither do I."

Her heartbeat sped up. "Then I don't understand why you're not kissing me right now."

Instead of answering, he got up and walked toward the window. She stared after him. A minute ago everything had been wonderful. How had this all gone so wrong so fast? She rose and followed him.

He had his back to her, looking out a window framing the sloping mountain that sparkled with the first golds and reds of autumn.

"The leaves are changing," she said. "I've been waiting for it, but I hadn't even noticed."

"Sometimes changes sneak up on us. Even things we're keeping an eye out for." He sighed. "Like this deal with us. I never saw myself getting married, Charlotte."

"It's a little late for that. You *are* married."

"You know what I mean. At the time, I told myself that was…an arrangement between friends." He turned to look at her. "The problem is, you're not only my best friend anymore, Charlotte. You're like…air to me now. Today, waiting here, not knowing where you were or if you'd even come back? I couldn't breathe." He shook his head. "It almost killed me."

"I'm sorry. I should have told you what I was planning to do. But you're right. I knew you'd want to go with me, and I knew I'd want to let you. This was something I needed to handle by myself."

"Why?"

"Because you'd already done enough. And because I needed to know I could handle it on my own." She tried to think of a way to explain. "You know Dylan hurt me."

Something flickered in his eyes. "Yes."

"That started after his drinking and gambling got out of control. Trouble doesn't always come from bad intentions, Logan. Sometimes it starts with somebody's weakness."

He kept his eyes on her face. "True enough."

"That's why I went to see Elizabeth without you. She'd always made me feel weak, but I had to prove to myself that I wasn't, that I could stand on my own two feet. Not just for myself, either, but for Daniel's sake, and yours. Does that make sense?"

"Maybe." He made a frustrated noise. "I don't know. I haven't been able to think straight since you kissed me." When she smiled, he added, "That's not a compliment."

"It sounds like one to me."

"Yeah, well. To me, it sounds like a problem."

Her heart dropped. Yes, she realized, for Logan, it might be. Trusting his feelings—or hers—would be harder for him than most. All his life, he'd survived by thinking things through, planning ahead, sticking to the straight and narrow.

And love could be a very curvy road.

After a second, he went on, "I've always tried to be honest with you."

It was such an understatement that she laughed. "I'll give you that."

"Then you know I'm being honest with you now. If we get married—"

"Logan, we already *are*—"

"I'm talking about really married. We'd do it again, here, with a minister, and my entire loud, we-told-you-so family—which is a good reason for you to think twice. We both need to be absolutely sure. You need to know that I'm not just another guy you feel sorry for because you think he's about to lose his job."

"That's not how I feel about you." She paused. "If that's what I need to know, what do you need to know?"

He studied her for a minute. "Whether or not I can breathe when you're gone, I guess."

"Logan—" She took a quick step toward him, but he held up a warning hand.

"If our feelings are strong enough to hold up a marriage—a real marriage—then they'll keep. You go on to Savannah." When she started to protest, he shook his head. "Don't, Charlotte. This isn't easy for me, either, and I don't have much willpower left. But you and I have seen enough marriages fall apart to know what's at stake here. For Danny and for us."

"I am sure." But the mention of Danny had its desired effect. He was right. She knew better than most what could happen when you made impulsive decisions. She had a child to consider now.

"Then go to Savannah." He ground out the words with some difficulty. "Settle up things there. Make some kind of peace with Elizabeth, if you can. Do whatever you need to do. Think things through. And...don't call me."

"What?" She stared at him, horrified. "Why not?"

"Because like I said, a man's only got so much will-power and I'm right at the end of mine. One phone conversation with you, and I'd be on the road to Savannah to bring you and Danny back here. Wait a few weeks, tend to your business. Pray. And when you're done, if you still want to, come back and we'll start planning a wedding."

"All right," she agreed slowly, hating what she was saying. "If that's how you want to do this, that's what we'll do." She took out her phone. "Elizabeth was going to stop for lunch. I'll ask her to drive Daniel and me back to Savannah today. The sooner I get there, the sooner I can get back."

For a minute she thought he was going to object, but then he nodded. "Maybe that's a good idea. You don't like driving the truck much, and that's a long haul. Plus, this way, if you decide to stay, you won't have to worry about returning it."

She looked up at him sharply. "I am coming back, Logan. I prom—"

"No. Don't make me any promises. Not yet." He sighed and squared his shoulders. "But hang on to them. Because if you do come back to me, I'm going to want them all."

Six weeks later, when the intercom buzzed for the fourth time in an hour, newly reelected Sheriff Logan Carter hurled his pen across the office. He was having an annoying afternoon, thanks to his persistent family—and a dispatcher who needed to learn how to follow orders.

He took a deep breath, reined in his temper and pressed the button.

"I said no calls, Marla."

"I know, but your sister's on line three." There was a nervous pause. "Again."

"Tell Maggie I'm busy."

"It's not Maggie this time. It's Torey, and she sounds annoyed."

His family had pulled out the big guns. Logan rubbed his forehead—hard. No wonder Marla was nervous. His dispatcher was used to dealing with your average, small-town lawbreakers. Torey was out of her league.

He'd have to handle this himself.

"Fine. I'll talk to her. But if any of them call back hang up on them. That's an order."

"Yes, sir." There was no mistaking the relief in Marla's voice.

He jabbed at the lighted button on the old phone. "The answer's no, Torey."

His sister didn't miss a beat. "It's your party, Logan. You have to come."

"I'm busy."

"Doing what?"

"Working."

Exasperated sigh. "You won the election. I think you can take an afternoon off."

He heard voices in the background. Sounded like a lot of people—the whole family, probably. He shoved aside a feeling of guilt.

This was not his fault, and he wasn't backing down.

"I think you don't understand how all this works. Winning the election gives me more responsibilities, not fewer. Besides, I said I didn't want a celebration party. I made that very clear. Several times. To everybody. Didn't I?"

"Yes, you did." One thing about Torey—she never flinched from the truth.

She never flinched, period. The woman was fearless.

"Then the fact that *somebody*," Maggie probably, but he wouldn't name names, "decided to throw one anyway isn't exactly my problem, is it?"

"It's going to be your problem if you don't show up."

"I don't negotiate with terrorists. You're not railroading me, Torey. Not this time. I'm not in the mood for a party. Period."

"Fine." Torey lowered her voice. "But everybody'll think it's because of Charlotte. You know that, right?"

It *was* because of Charlotte. Six weeks, and no word. It was taking every bit of his self-control not to jump in his car, hit the lights and sirens and head to Savannah.

He hadn't and he wouldn't. But he knew that was why his family was being so bullheaded about this silly party. They wanted him to cheer up.

But he wasn't in a party mood, and he didn't appreciate being lied to, even when the intentions were kind.

"They can think whatever they want. Sorry, Torey. I was promised no party, and I'm holding you all to it."

There was a long, heavy pause. "You should come, Logan."

There was something in his sister's voice…he couldn't put his finger on it, but it didn't ring quite right. "Why?"

"Because I said so."

Nice try. "Last time I checked I didn't answer to you."

"Because Ruby said so, then."

"Did she?"

There was a rustling noise, and he heard his foster mom's voice. "You'd best come on home, son."

"See?" Torey came back on the phone, a note of triumph in her voice. "So?"

He chewed the inside of his cheek. "I'll come by after work."

"That's four hours from now!"

"Four hours if I don't end up working late. That's the best I can do. And, Torey? Don't call back."

He hung up the phone and rummaged in his desk drawer for another pen.

His family meant well. They'd been fussing over him for weeks now. That was his fault, he guessed. He'd been walking around in a daze, jumping whenever his phone rang.

It had never been the call he was hoping for. The longer Charlotte's silence had lasted, the worse he'd felt.

Silence spoke pretty loudly sometimes.

A now-familiar ache started up, and he cleared his throat and turned his attention to the forms on his desk. Barton Myers had launched an impressive smear campaign, based on Marty Carter's criminal history, but it hadn't worked. Logan had won the election by a landslide. That was something. He needed to focus on his job, and the first order of business was outlining some ideas for the afterschool boys' mentoring program he planned to start.

His mind went to Danny, and he chewed hard on the inside of his cheek. Once things had…settled down some… he'd get in touch with Charlotte. He'd make arrangements to see Danny, if she'd agree. Surely, she would. He'd given his word he'd be there for the kid, and she knew how seriously he took that.

Half an hour later there was a commotion in the lobby. He tilted his head and listened—his frown deepening.

He should've expected this. Torey never took no for an answer.

He rose to his feet and waited until the door opened.

"I told you—" he started.

It wasn't Torey.

Charlotte stood in front of him, wearing a shimmery golden dress that fluttered halfway between her knees and her ankles. It was one of her designs. He knew that without being told, recognized her personality in the lines of it.

With a twining brown vine bearing round red berries braided into her hair, she reminded him of the woods just before winter set in. Just when you thought all the autumn beauty had faded away, you'd stumble across some hidden pocket of loveliness, all the prettier because it was unexpected.

"Surprise," she said softly.

His brain had given up and shut down. All he could think of to say was, "What's going on?"

"I came to get you." She came closer. Behind her, he saw Marla and three of his deputies crowding in the doorway, their eyes wide. "Torey says you're being stubborn."

"Stubborn."

"Very." She tilted her head. "It's not polite, you know, skipping out on your own party when everybody's gone to so much trouble."

"Party." He couldn't do anything but repeat words and stare at her.

"Well, wedding, actually. Although, making the bride drag you there herself…" She twinkled a smile at him. "Not good form, Sheriff."

He dropped into his chair with a thump. "Bride?"

"That would be me." Charlotte kept her eyes on his. "Like I said. Surprise."

"Marla, shut the door." He waited until she complied, then got up and walked around the desk, his full attention on Charlotte. "Maybe you'd better fill me in."

"We'll have to make it quick. The minister's waiting, and Daniel will be getting hungry soon. Wait until you see him, Logan! He's grown so much, you won't believe it!"

"I want to see him. It's killed me, missing him. And you." He paused. "It's been six weeks, Charlotte."

"I know." Her voice thrummed with the same pain he'd been feeling. "Six weeks that felt like forever. But I did what you asked, Logan. I went to Savannah, and I wrapped up all the details of my life there, as best I could. Then I waited until the election was over. Congratulations, by the way."

"Thanks."

"But just so we're clear, I was planning to show up in this dress whether you won or not."

She spoke so fiercely that he had to grin. "Fair enough. Now maybe you'd better clue me in on this wedding that I know nothing about."

She smiled. "Kind of throws you off when somebody plans your wedding without telling you, doesn't it? I should know. You did the same thing to me."

"No." He took another step, closing the gap between them. "If I'm understanding you right, this isn't the same thing at all. Am I understanding you right?"

"I don't know." He was so close now, that she had to tip her face up to look at him. "It's been six weeks, Logan. So tell me," she held his gaze, "were you able to breathe while I was gone?"

He shook his head. "No," he murmured roughly. "No, I wasn't."

He put his arms around her, pulled her close. He watched her, waiting, but she didn't flinch, didn't pull back. Instead, she raised one hand and laid it lightly against his cheek.

"I'm glad to hear it," she said.

So he kissed her. Six long weeks of worry and waiting were in that kiss, but she only curved herself closer and kissed him back.

When they finally pulled apart, he told her the truth, just like he always had. Plain and simple.

"I love you, Charlotte."

The smile that dawned across her face brightened the room. "I love you, too. I'd planned on telling you that in front of a minister and a big, loud, I-told-you-so family, wearing this really pretty dress. But it seems my groom isn't willing to take the afternoon off."

"He's reconsidering. And you aren't the only one who's been doing some planning." He took her left hand and drew the plain gold band off her finger. Reaching behind the desk, he yanked open a drawer and dropped it in.

"Logan, we're going to need that."

"No, we aren't." Pulling out the velvet box he'd tucked in there four weeks ago, he cracked it open.

He heard her soft murmur as she saw the engagement ring and wedding band he'd commissioned the day after she'd left. His brother Ryder had known a guy, a jeweler specializing in custom rings.

Ryder always knew a guy. But this time, his guy had come through. Made of silver and gold twisted gracefully together, both rings were engraved with tiny, delicate blooms and leaves. That and the inscription inside were their only decoration.

No diamonds, he'd told the man. Nothing cold, nothing too traditional. He'd wanted something special, something unique and artistic, something like Charlotte herself.

"Logan, they're beautiful," she whispered. "They're perfect. But you didn't have to—"

"Yes, I did. We're starting over, and this time we're doing everything right. Will you marry me?" Her eyebrows went up teasingly, so he added with a sigh, "Again?"

He noticed everything about Charlotte. He always had. So he saw the promise in her eyes before she gave it, before she said the word he'd had engraved on the inside of her ring weeks ago.

"Always."

Epilogue

"It's going to storm tonight," Ruby announced to the family who'd assembled to celebrate her birthday one cold January evening. "First heavy snow of the winter."

Logan glanced at Charlotte, seated beside him at the kitchen table holding Daniel. Since becoming sheriff, he'd lost his appreciation for snow. Georgia drivers weren't used to the stuff, and it caused problems on his roads.

This year, though, a good, old-fashioned snowstorm didn't sound half bad. The roads would still be a pain, but after work, he'd be cozying up with his new family while the wind whispered around their snug cabin.

He liked that idea.

"Sounds like a good excuse to build a fire," he said to his wife. "I'll do that as soon as we get back home."

"An evening snuggled up with you in front of the fireplace? Sounds perfect." Charlotte smiled, and as usual, his heart turned to mush. After a full month of their marriage-for-keeps, he'd expected that to have slowed down some.

It hadn't. He was starting to think it never would. And that was fine by him.

"Dial it down, you nauseating lovebirds. Some of us are eating here." Ryder checked the weather app on his phone as he scooped up another bite of Maggie's caramel cake. "Nope, Ruby. Weatherman says the storm's going to miss us. No snow in the forecast."

Ruby snorted. "That city weatherman hasn't lived in these mountains for over seventy years. A big snow's coming—I'm telling you. I feel it in my bones."

"And there's no arguing with Ruby's bones." Maggie made a playful face at Danny before gathering up the plates. "I'm jealous, Charlotte. I miss the fires in that big stone fireplace." She threw her husband a lingering glance. "So romantic."

"Still eating," Ryder pointed out. Maggie bopped him on the head as she passed by.

"You'll need that fire, likely," Ruby said. "You ain't weathered a real storm in that cabin yet, Logan. It's set higher up so it's a good bit more exposed than this old farm. Cold gets fierce up there. I expect you'll be needing extra covers for your bed, too."

"I doubt it," Logan said absently. His mind was on Charlotte, and how beautiful she'd look with firelight playing over her sweet face. "Those log walls are so thick—"

"Your mom's right, Logan," Charlotte interrupted, and he shot her a puzzled look.

"'Course I'm right. And I have just the thing. I been waiting for the right time to give it to you. Go get that big bag there, Jina." When his youngest sister snagged the oversize gift sack, Ruby nodded at him, her worn face bright with expectation. "Now give it to your big brother."

The decorated paper bag was heavy and oddly soft. "Why am I getting a present? Today's your birthday, Ruby, not mine."

"Since it's my day, I can give gifts to whoever I want to, can't I? Although that one there is from me and Charlotte both. Go on, son. Open it up."

He glanced at his wife. "This is what you and Ruby have been working on?"

She smiled. "Yes. It took longer than we'd thought, but we finally finished it."

"Just in time, too," Ruby muttered. "No matter what that fool weatherman thinks."

Logan tossed aside tufts of tissue paper and lifted out a thick square of material. He stood carefully back from the crumb-littered table and unfolded it. His siblings made awed noises and broke out into spontaneous applause.

His memory quilt—a large one with strong colors, sporting a huge star in the middle, pieced together in various shades of gold. Smaller stars decorated the corners.

He didn't know much about quilts, but even he knew this one was stunning. The overall design was traditional and bold, but he saw telltale signs of Charlotte's creative quirkiness. The bordering stars were tilted and very slightly off-center, and the strips running up and down the sides of the quilt were made of familiar-looking bits of material, oddly shaped but well matched, fitting together perfectly.

Kind of reminded him of the people around this table, come to think of it.

"That's gorgeous," Maggie whispered. Murmurs of agreement came from the others.

Even Ryder whistled under his breath, examining a corner of the quilt with a salesman's critical eye. "It's amazing, that's what it is. I don't know much about textile art, but I know this—Charlotte, if you want to go in business making these things, I can sell them for you all day long."

Logan glanced at his wife. She looked thoughtful. "That's an idea. I'd like to start sewing professionally again. Not for fancy weddings," she added. "But quilts like this one might be interesting. Traditional, but with modern twist."

"Sign me up as your first customer," Ryder said.

"Don't you worry, son." Ruby shot him a speculative glance. "You'll be getting a quilt of your own real soon. I been doing a lot of thinking about you just lately."

Torey poked her brother. "You know what that means. You're next on her matchmaking list."

Ryder looked alarmed. "If that quilt comes with a wife, count me out. No offense, Charlotte, but marriage isn't in my plans."

Ruby made an impatient noise. "Wasn't in Logan's plans either. Nor Maggie's, as I recall. Plans change."

"Mine aren't going to, so don't get your hopes up."

"Ain't about me getting my hopes up, son. It's about you getting yours up, taking those plans of yours and making them into something better. Like this quilt here. It proves my point real well. Those shirts of Logan's were so old and worn-out. They looked kind of bad."

"Most of them looked bad when they were new," Torey murmured. She caught her older brother's eye and shrugged. "You always want the truth. That's the truth."

"But—" Ruby went on with her impromptu sermon, shooting her middle daughter a sharp look "—me and Charlotte took the best bits and put them together into something strong and lasting. You two will pass this here quilt down to your grandchildren, and it'll be a real blessing to them. And this ain't nothing. Try handing those raggedy plans of yours over to the Lord, and see what He can do. You never know. He might add in a pretty new piece that pulls everything together real well."

She nodded at Maggie and Neil, seated with Gracie, Oliver and their two foster children, Josh and Margot. Then she smiled at Logan, Charlotte and baby Daniel. Finally her glance slid to Ryder, and she winked.

"Mark my words," she said, "you'll be finding that out for yourself pretty soon. I feel it in my bones."

"Uh-oh." Ryder looked stricken, and everybody laughed.

Everybody except for Logan, who was gazing at Charlotte as she laughed comfortably with their family. And when Neil darted past her to rescue a glass that Oliver had set teetering on the table edge, she didn't even flinch.

She wasn't afraid anymore. She was beaming, beautiful and happy.

And his.

What they had between them would last, too. Like the mountains sheltering this old farm, like this quilt that would pass down not only to his grandchildren but to his great-grandchildren.

He knew it.

Logan had looked for truth all his life, he'd dedicated himself to it, and he recognized it when he saw it. This unexpected love he and Charlotte had pieced together from friendship and heartache and hope would endure.

"For always," he murmured.

His wife-for-keeps glanced up, giving him the special smile that belonged only to him.

"Always," she whispered back. Then she nestled in close, settling her head against his shoulder. And outside Ruby's kitchen window the first snowflakes began to fall.

* * * * *

*If you enjoyed this story, don't miss
Laurel Blount's next sweet romance,
available next year from Love Inspired!*

Find more great reads at www.LoveInspired.com

Dear Reader,

Welcome back to Cedar Ridge, Georgia—a small mountain town with a great big heart!

After *Lost and Found Faith*, many readers reached out, curious about Ruby's matchmaking plans for her oldest foster son, Sheriff Logan Carter, and I'm so excited to share his story.

This is my first book featuring a hero in law enforcement. I'm delighted to have the opportunity to showcase the integrity and selfless dedication these officers so often exhibit. The fine men and women who serve their communities honorably—like Logan—deserve much appreciation and support.

I hope you enjoyed this return visit to Cedar Ridge because Ruby's not done yet! Now she's got her matchmaking eye on her foster son Ryder Montgomery—and this marriage-is-not-for-me bachelor may be her toughest job so far!

In the meantime, let's keep in touch! Head over to www.laurelblountbooks.com and sign up to be a part of my favorite bunch of folks—my beloved newsletter subscribers! Every month I share photos, giveaways, book news and gotta-try-it recipes. And of course, you can always write me directly at laurelblountwrites@gmail.com. I look forward to hearing from you!

Much love,
Laurel

LOVE INSPIRED

Stories to uplift and inspire

Fall in love with Love Inspired—
inspirational and uplifting stories of faith
and hope. Find strength and comfort in
the bonds of friendship and community.
Revel in the warmth of possibility and the
promise of new beginnings.

Sign up for the Love Inspired newsletter
at **LoveInspired.com** to be the first
to find out about upcoming titles,
special promotions and exclusive content.

SPECIAL EXCERPT FROM

LOVE INSPIRED
INSPIRATIONAL ROMANCE

*With her emotional support dog at her side,
Jalissa Tucker will do whatever it takes to ensure the
survival of the local animal rescue—even ally herself
with her nemesis, firefighter Jeremy Rider. As working
together dredges up old hurts, putting the past aside
could be the key to their future joy...*

Read on for a sneak preview of
An Unlikely Alliance *by Toni Shiloh,
available July 2022 from Love Inspired!*

What are you thinking?

Apparently, she wasn't. Jalissa straightened her shoulders and slipped her mental armor on. Just because Rider had been perfectly charming with her family didn't mean she'd let that soften her toward him. He was still arrogant, immature and a touch reckless.

"Morning, Tucker," Rider said when he opened her door. "Captain Simms's wife is already here and has set up the perfect spot for the shoot." Rider pointed toward the rear of the van. "Animals in the back?"

"Yes. They're all in crates."

He opened the back doors then shook his head. "How did you survive the ride with all that noise?"

"Found my happy place." And one day she'd see Hawaii in person. She loosened Flo and moved back so the dog could exit the van through the driver's side.

"You know what happiness is?" Rider smirked.

"Hardy har-har." Jalissa rounded the back to start unloading the animals. "Where am I putting them?"

"Oh, don't worry about it." Rider cupped his mouth. "Young, Trent, Barns, come help!"

She wiggled a finger in her eardrum. "I think your voice carries well enough without you shouting."

"Maybe, but I have no idea where they are in the firehouse. Now you don't have to carry the animals. Plus, the guys already know where everything is set up."

"Then I can leave?" She had a load of laundry she could do.

"Oh, no." He tsked at her. "We need your assistance with the animals."

Jalissa slowly inched backward but stopped when Flo nudged her. *One…two…* She could do this. Be near the firehouse for help. She didn't actually have to go *inside*, did she? Flo licked her fingertips.

"All right," Jalissa said slowly. "I'll just stay out of everyone's way unless I'm needed."

"You'll be needed." He stared into her eyes.

She blinked slowly. What was going on with her? First thinking Rider was good-looking, and now they were having some kind of moment. She needed to fix this real quick. "I'm sure. It's not like I can trust you to be competent."

The firemen rounded the back of the van, ignoring her conversation with Rider. They quietly began unloading the crates.

Rider rocked back on his heels, sliding his hands into his pockets. "Shots fired in, what?" He pulled an arm up to glance at his watch. "Five minutes. Must be some kind of record for you."

"Whatever." She gave him a wide berth and followed the last fireman from the side parking lot to the front of the firehouse.

She inhaled. *One…two…three…four…* Exhale. *Five…six… seven…eight…* Flo bumped into her hand as if to let Jalissa know she wasn't alone. She buried her fingers in the soft fur as they strolled up the walkway.

Don't miss
An Unlikely Alliance *by Toni Shiloh,*
available July 2022
wherever Love Inspired books and ebooks are sold.

LoveInspired.com

LIEXP0522

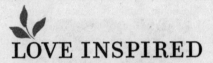

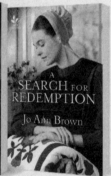

When a cold-case serial killer returns, FBI special agent Fiona Kelly has one last chance to stop him before he claims the prize he's always wanted—*her*.

Don't miss this thrilling and uplifting page-turner
from bestselling author

JESSICA R. PATCH

"*Her Darkest Secret* by Jessica R. Patch grabbed me in the first scene of this edge-of-your-seat suspense and didn't let go until the end!"
—**Patricia Bradley**, author of the Memphis Cold Case novels

Available now from Love Inspired!